Christmas Captive

Jane Blythe

Copyright © 2018 Jane Blythe

All rights reserved.

No part of this publication may be reproduced, transmitted, downloaded, distributed, reverse engineered or stored in or introduced into any information storage and retrieval system, in any form or by any means, including photocopying and recording, whether electronic or mechanical, now known or hereinafter invented without permission in writing from the publisher.

All characters and events in this publication, other than those clearly in the public domain, are fictitious and any resemblance to real persons, living or dead, is purely coincidental.

Bear Spots Publications
Melbourne Australia

bearspotspublications@gmail.com

Paperback
ISBN: 0-6484033-2-7
ISBN-13: 978-0-6484033-2-6

Cover designed by QDesigns

Also by Jane Blythe

Detective Parker Bell Series

A SECRET TO THE GRAVE
WINTER WONDERLAND
DEAD OR ALIVE
LITTLE GIRL LOST
FORGOTTEN

Count to Ten Series

ONE
TWO
THREE
FOUR
FIVE
SIX

Christmas Romantic Suspense Series

CHRISTMAS HOSTAGE
CHRISTMAS CAPTIVE

I'd like to thank everyone who played a part in bringing this story to life. Particularly my mom who is always there to share her thoughts and opinions with me. My awesome cover designer, Amy, who whips up covers for me so quickly and who patiently makes every change I ask for, and there are usually lots of them! And my lovely editor Mitzi Carroll, and proofreader Marisa Nichols, for all their encouragement and for all the hard work they put into polishing my work.

DECEMBER 18TH

8:23 P.M.

She was out of breath.

Taylor didn't think she could keep running much longer.

But she couldn't stop either.

So, she ran, praying she could get far enough away before he came for her. She was sure he must know that she was gone by now. He could be looking for her.

That thought was enough to keep her pushing through the pain to keep moving.

With each step, her right leg throbbed like it was on fire. It was too soon to be running on the broken bone, but it wasn't like she had a choice. She could do nothing and stay where she was and wait like a good little girl to be murdered, or she could run for her life; and if she caused her body more damage in the process, at least she'd be alive.

It was dark out and cold. She thought about flagging down one of the cars whose headlights periodically bathed her in light, but she was afraid. What if it was *him*? Taylor knew he'd be looking for her; she was his prize possession and he wouldn't want to give her up until he was finished with her.

She didn't know where she was going.

She didn't know when she was going to stop running.

If it were possible to never stop, then she would probably keep running for the rest of her life. It felt so good to be able to move freely again after so long in that tiny room. All this open space around her was both exhilarating and terrifying. In a way, she had become used to her room, as much as she hated it. It had offered some weird sort of comfort. She knew what to expect, she knew when to expect it, and she knew what she had to do to survive.

Now she was free.

Anything could happen to her.

The man might jump out and grab her at any second. He could be waiting around any corner. He could be lurking behind any car or tree she passed. He could be following along behind her just waiting for her to stop so he could pounce.

Or she could go running into the arms of another bad man. There were so many out there. She'd never thought about it before; her life had always been so safe, so controlled, so peaceful. Although she knew there were evil people in the world and that people were hurt every single day, it never felt real because it'd never touched her personally.

Now, it did.

Now she had been initiated into the darkness.

She could never go back.

Her life would never be the same.

The pain in her leg was intensifying with each step she took. Her breath was wheezing in and out—she hadn't exercised in months, and she was out of shape. She was also starting to feel a little light-headed. She probably wasn't going to be able to keep going much longer, and then what?

What would she do?

Should she try to hide?

That didn't seem like much of a long-term solution. She couldn't hide forever. She needed to eat, and it was cold out. Besides, hiding in some small, stuffy little space felt too much like returning to the very situation she had just escaped.

Should she try to find help?

Right now, Taylor couldn't imagine trusting a stranger enough to go up to them and tell them what had happened to her and ask them to drive her to the nearest police station.

Maybe she should look for a police station herself.

Or even a hospital or a fire station would do.

If she knew where she was, she could try to get to one of her friends' houses or maybe even her brother's.

Her pace was slowing. Now she was doing more fast walking than slow running. To anyone who saw her she couldn't look like she was just out for an evening walk or jog because she was wearing an ankle-length, white cotton dress, and her feet were bare. It was clear she didn't belong out here on this icy cold night dressed like this, and yet no one stopped to help her.

Taylor wasn't sure if that was a good thing or bad.

Knowing her luck, anyone who stopped to help her would be some creep driving around on a winter's night looking for a vulnerable woman to prey upon.

Winter.

It was winter, or close enough to it. There was a light dusting of snow over everything and the sidewalk under her feet was cold enough that it felt like stepping on a million tiny shards of glass. It would have hurt if she had time to worry about such things.

As she continued to slow, she noticed that yards were decorated with fairy lights and elaborate Christmas displays. Some of the houses she passed had Christmas trees in their windows.

Christmastime.

It seemed so surreal. For her, the world had stopped the day she'd been taken, but for everyone else, it had moved as usual. While she'd been held prisoner, people had been going about their lives.

Her cheeks began to sting, and she knew it was because she was crying.

Life was so unfair.

Why had he chosen her?

There was nothing special about her. She was just a normal woman. At twenty years old, she worked as a hairdresser, went to college, and hung out with her friends. She had dinner with her parents and younger brother every other week, went shopping, owned way too many pairs of shoes, and had an addiction to donuts that required daily trips to the gym to work off the extra calories. There was nothing about her that should have put her in the sights of that horrible man.

He could have chosen any one of the thousands of young women her age. Instead, he had taken her.

She again slowed; her legs were shaking so badly she was surprised she was still standing.

She was fueled by pure adrenaline, but that could only last so long.

Then she would likely collapse in the middle of the street.

If she did, she would be completely vulnerable. Anyone could stumble upon her and do whatever they wanted to her. She would be at their mercy.

She needed a plan.

She needed to make up her mind what she was going to do.

Anything was better than the prospect of passing out on the sidewalk.

Maybe she should flag down the next car that passed.

Maybe she should approach the nearest house.

Maybe she should start looking for a safe place to go for help.

She did none of those things.

She just kept moving.

Somehow, she continued to propel herself forward.

Her vision was beginning to blur. Each breath she took was a harsh pant, her bad leg wobbled, and her stomach was churning now with a mixture of anxiety and overexertion.

The sound of a car approaching had her head snapping up.

Headlights were bearing down on her.

Taking the biggest leap of faith in her life, she stumbled out onto the road. Waving her arms above her head, she prayed the person in the car wouldn't hurt her. After what she'd been through, her faith in humanity had taken a severe beating. She was no longer that sweet, innocent girl who always saw the best in people—now she expected the worst.

The car approached. Once the driver noticed her, the vehicle swerved wildly, almost crashing into an illuminated Santa in a sleigh that decorated the closest front yard.

Instead of stopping, tires squealed, and the car took off down the street.

They hadn't stopped.

It took a moment for that to sink in.

They had probably thought she was just some drunk.

Tears burned her eyes.

She had nowhere to go. She didn't want to stop moving, but no doubt that was about to happen any second now. She'd probably be found dead by the side of the road come morning.

At least it would be a quick death. She wouldn't have to suffer anymore.

Maybe that was for the best.

Death would relieve her from her torment.

Death would be peace and quiet.

Death would be the ultimate freedom.

It seemed unfair that she had escaped hell only to die anyway, surrounded by help she was too afraid to seek. Taylor was in a residential area; she could go up to one of the houses, but that seemed like playing roulette with her life. If she picked the wrong house, she could wind up in an even worse position than the one she had just fled.

"What should I do?" she cried aloud.

Surely, she wasn't going to let fear beat her now. Not after how hard she fought to keep hold of her sanity and her soul, not after everything she had done to get herself here. To give up now would be weak—pathetic, even.

She could do this.

Picking a house at random, she staggered toward it.

It looked safe enough. It was a brick ranch, an inflatable carousel in the front yard with a snowman, a Santa, an elf, and a gingerbread man riding reindeer in place of horses. If someone had chosen something that cute to decorate their yard, how bad could they be?

Battling her fears, Taylor stepped toward the house and then screamed when a pair of arms wrapped around her.

* * * * *

9:08 P.M.

Fin Patrick held the screaming woman tighter when she tried to fight her way out of his arms.

He was surprised she had the strength to fight as vehemently as she was. He'd seen her earlier, stumbling down the street, almost getting hit by a car when she'd staggered out onto the road. He had assumed she was drunk and had been about to run into the road to pull her out of harm's way, but thankfully the driver of the car had seen her and swerved to miss her.

After that, Fin had turned away, assuming the woman was going to find her way to her house and get herself indoors. She really should; she wasn't dressed to be outside on a winter night.

But then the woman had headed for his house. He had no idea why, but for the first time, he began to get an inkling that something was wrong. The woman looked like she was barely able to remain on her feet. He was worried about her. What if she had mixed drugs with alcohol?

"Stop squirming," he said firmly. "I'm not going to hurt you."

She didn't seem to hear him. Her struggling intensified, her chest heaved against his arm, and Fin could feel small drops of cold liquid falling on his hands.

The woman was crying.

Maybe she wasn't wandering home drunk from a Christmas party as he'd thought; maybe she was a victim of an assault. That could explain why she wasn't properly dressed, her seemingly drugged state and the fact that she was freaking out at his touch.

He released his hold on the woman but kept his arms out in case her legs gave way. "It's all right," Fin said, trying to keep his voice soothing. "I'm not going to hurt you."

Wild eyes frantically scanned her surroundings.

Up close, she didn't look drunk or drugged; she looked terrified. The possibility that she had just been assaulted seemed more and more likely.

"Ma'am, can you tell me your name?"

Large green eyes finally landed on him, and she took a step back, swaying unsteadily.

He obviously wasn't reassuring her, and he didn't know what to say or do to put her at ease.

"My name's Fin," he told her. "Dr. Fin Patrick."

She went still.

He wasn't sure if that was a good thing or not. Hearing he was a doctor was either enough to engender trust or freak her out more.

"D-doctor?" she repeated.

"At the hospital ... I work in the ER," he elaborated. It seemed like the knowledge he was a doctor was comforting to her. "And you are?" he prompted.

"Taylor. Taylor Sallow." Although she hadn't bolted and did indeed seem reassured now, she hadn't relaxed. Her eyes still roved back and forth behind him as though she suspected a monster to come crashing in at any second. If he was right and she had been attacked, he needed to know. It might not be safe for her here, but Fin was wary of attempting to take her inside; she was likely to freak out again at the prospect of being alone in a house with a stranger.

"Are you all right, Taylor?" He gave her an assessing once-over. Even in the thin light of the streetlight, he could see that she was very pale; it didn't look like she spent much time outdoors. There was a small smudge of what he thought was blood on the inside of her right elbow. She stood with most of her weight on one leg, her other she held stiffly like it caused her pain. He needed to know what injuries she had and how bad they were.

She hadn't answered his question, and she still looked unsure about whether or not she could trust him. He wanted to assure her that she could, but how could he do that? Taylor was obviously afraid, and anything he did or said could scare her even more. She had answered his direct question, but not his open-ended one, so perhaps if he focused more on yes or no questions, he would have a better chance of getting information out of her.

"Is your leg hurt, Taylor?"

"Broken," she murmured.

If it was broken, it wasn't a recent break—there was no way she'd be able to walk on it like she had been when he'd first seen her. But if it wasn't recent, then how did that fit in with what had happened to her? "And your arm?"

She followed his gaze to the small patch of blood on her dress and gave a small nod.

"Did someone hurt you, Taylor?"

She had calmed a little, but her breathing was still ragged. "Yes."

"Are you running from him?"

"Yes."

With her admission, the last of her energy dissipated, it seemed to be the only thing keeping her on her feet and as it disappeared she pitched forward. Fin moved and caught her before she hit the ground.

He had intended to just steady her, maybe ease her down, so she was sitting, sure that her reaction to his touch would be the same as it had been before. But this time she didn't fight him. She didn't struggle. She didn't recoil; instead, she curled into him, wrapping her thin arms around his neck and pressing her small body against him.

"I ... I hit him, and ... and I ran ... he must know I'm gone

... he'll be looking for me. I ran for as long as I could ... but I don't know how far I came," she said brokenly. Her tears were back, and she cried quietly into his shoulder.

If what she'd said was true, and Fin had no doubt that it was, then he needed to get her someplace safe. The man who'd hurt her could have followed her here. He could be lurking nearby. He could even randomly stumble upon them if he was searching for his lost captive.

First things first. He had to calm down the weeping girl in his arms enough that she would let him bundle her into his car and drive her straight to the hospital. He'd just come home from his shift when he'd seen her floundering on the sidewalk, and he hadn't expected to be going back there so quickly, but he couldn't turn this woman away. She couldn't be more than twenty-two maybe twenty-three, she was injured—someone had hurt her— and he couldn't just turn his back, ignore her, and walk away. He needed to see her safely to the hospital, then call the cops and let them handle things.

She was shivering in his arms, her thin dress offering no protection from the cold, and her feet were bare. She was no doubt suffering mild hypothermia, especially if she'd been out here for any length of time. Fin was wearing a coat over the hospital scrubs, so he shrugged out of it and wrapped it around her, unhooking her arms from around his neck and sliding them into the sleeves, then easing her off his chest so he could button it up.

"I'm just going to check your vitals," he informed Taylor as he reached for her wrist. He took her pulse, found it racing, no doubt from panic and running for her life. His stethoscope was still around his neck. He often forgot about it and wore it for hours, sometimes even falling asleep with it on, finding it buried under the covers in the morning. He listened to her chest. Her lungs sounded clear, her heart was pounding, and he wondered if it was just fear that had it racing or whether she hadn't exerted any sort of major energy in a long time. He still didn't know the details of what she'd been through. Who had taken her? When? How long had she been with her attacker? What else had he done to her? As much as he wanted answers to all of those questions, they weren't his priority right now.

It was time for them to move. Taylor's injuries didn't appear to be too serious, although he'd make sure her leg was properly examined. It wasn't her medical condition that had him on edge, it was her safety. The longer they stayed here, the more danger she was in.

Fin didn't quite like the idea of getting mixed up in whatever had happened to Taylor, but for the moment, there wasn't much he could do about it. He would help her. It was the right thing to do, but he had no intention of waiting here for some lunatic to come and reclaim his victim, most likely killing anyone who got in his way.

"Taylor." He stroked her back in an attempt to soothe her. "Will you let me take you to the hospital?"

Immediately, she tensed.

The idea of going anywhere with him was obviously a terrifying one.

Whatever she had been through had no doubt been traumatic, but he didn't have time for hysterics right now. Both of their lives depended on getting somewhere safe.

"Do you still want to be here if he comes?"

Her head shook against his shoulder.

"Don't you want to go somewhere safe?"

A nod.

"Then let me take you to the hospital. You'll be safe there, and we can call the police. They'll be able to help you and find the man who hurt you, so you can remain safe. That's what you want, isn't it?"

Taylor paused for a moment, then nodded.

Taking that as her assent, Fin put one arm under her knees, the other around her shoulders, and lifted her up. He gave a quick glance around, and when he saw nothing out of place, he carried her to his car, managing to unlock it and open the door without dropping his still weeping bundle, and deposited her in the passenger seat.

She made no move to buckle her seatbelt, so he did it for her before going around and getting in the driver's seat. Although he half expected the boogeyman to come jumping out at any moment, the drive to the hospital was uneventful. He drove and Taylor cried. Fin hoped that the girl had a strong family unit to help her deal with whatever she had been through. He knew better than most the struggle of dealing with tragedy on your own.

Parking in front of the hospital, he was ready to deliver the girl into the care of someone else, then go home and return to battling through the worst Christmas season of his life.

*****

10:37 P.M.

This was not how she had envisioned her evening turning out.

Special Agent Chloe Luckman had intended to spend the evening in bed, crying, until she wore herself out and finally fell into a fitful sleep she knew would be full of bad dreams. She had done a lot of crying in the last seven months. She tried to be strong, to keep it together, to convince everyone that she had moved on and that she was doing okay, but alone in bed at night she couldn't keep up the act. Her mask cracked, and her pain came pouring out.

She'd thought it would be better by now.

Seven months should be long enough to feel like she didn't have to cry herself to sleep each night. It should be enough that she had come to terms with what happened and learned to deal with it. It wasn't like she could change it, so she had no choice but to accept it. It was just *so* hard.

Work was her salvation right now. It was pretty much the only thing that kept her getting out of bed each morning.

It was work that had her here at the hospital at nearly eleven at night, and she was thankful for the distraction. It never lasted long; the pain always crept back into the forefront of her mind; but when she was focused on something else, it hovered in the background.

Chloe wasn't paying attention to what she was doing or where she was going and walked straight into someone.

"Whoa," the person said as they grabbed hold of her biceps to stop her falling as she bounced off them.

The voice was one she recognized. One she had come to know quite well in the last seven months. One that had comforted her more times than she could count.

"Chloe." He sounded surprised to see her. "What are you doing here?"

"Work," she replied.

"Oh, you're working Taylor Sallow's case."

"You are too?" she asked Dr. Eric Abbott.

"I just finished examining her."

"How is she?"

"Mild hypothermia and a partially healed broken bone in her leg. Other than that, she's in reasonable physical condition."

That was good news, but it wasn't the young woman's physical condition she was most concerned about. "What about psychologically?"

"Traumatized," Eric summarized. "She hasn't spoken much since she was brought here. I tried engaging her while I was examining her, but she just lay there and looked at me. She's obviously afraid, which makes sense if we're correct in our assumptions of what happened to her."

Chloe agreed. Taylor Sallow had disappeared almost nineteen months ago, and they believed they knew where she'd been in those missing months. If they were right, and they wouldn't know until Taylor herself gave them confirmation, then the young woman had suffered horribly.

"How are *you* doing?" Eric asked, changing the subject.

She didn't want to lie to the doctor who had become her friend over the last several months, but she also didn't want to get into a discussion about her mental health. She had met Eric seven months ago when she had been in a horrible car accident, and he had been her doctor.

That would have been the extent of their relationship if it hadn't been for what they had in common.

In the car accident she hadn't been seriously injured, but the injuries she'd had, had been life-changing. She had been five months pregnant, and she'd gone into premature labor. At only twenty weeks, the baby wasn't viable and had lived only a couple of minutes before dying in her arms.

There hadn't been a day that had gone by since that she hadn't missed her son. If he hadn't died and she'd carried him to term, he'd be almost four months old now, babbling and rolling over and maybe getting his first tooth. Chloe knew she'd never get over his loss but hoped the pain would begin to dull with time. She couldn't survive with this slicing agony in her heart indefinitely.

Eric Abbott and his wife Lila had lost their five-year-old son in a carjacking. He'd been shot, lost too much blood, and didn't survive. According to Eric, their son's death had almost destroyed his marriage and his wife. But over time, they had learned to draw strength from one another instead of pulling away from each other. Now, close to a decade later, their relationship was stronger than ever, and he and Lila had added another two children to their family.

She and Eric had talked a lot about the loss of a child. Although the circumstances of their losses were vastly different, the pain was the same. She had drawn comfort from his words and the fact that he'd managed to find happiness even though the pain of his son's death would never leave him.

It gave her hope that one day she would find herself in the same place.

"Have you talked to him?" Eric asked.

"Who?" She feigned innocence. Her baby wasn't the only thing she had lost after the accident.

"You know who."

"No."

"I know you've said no the last few times I've brought it up—"

"And I'm going to say no again this time," she interrupted.

"But I really think," Eric continued, undaunted, "that you should talk to someone."

"I don't need a shrink," she huffed.

"My brother is really good. Seriously. I'm not just saying that because he's my brother. Charlie has helped a lot of people. A lot of people who were a lot more adamant than you are that they didn't need help. Just think about it. Please. I don't want to see you go down a path that you don't know how to find your way back from."

Eric looked so sincere that she found herself wanting to say yes just to make him feel better.

Chloe might well have done it if she hadn't seen her partner come rushing through the hospital's doors. She and Tom Drake had been partners for a little over a year now, and she considered him and his wife close friends. She had learned a lot from Tom. He'd helped her become a better agent, and he had been very supportive following the loss of her son.

"Sorry I'm late," Tom said as he hurried over to join them. While Chloe spent most of her time in bed crying when she wasn't at work, Tom also spent most of his time in bed only for a whole different reason. Her partner had reconnected with his ex-wife a year ago, and the two were about the sappiest, most in love couple she had ever seen.

Sometimes Chloe couldn't quite help the little stab of jealousy she felt when she saw Tom and Hannah together. It wasn't that she begrudged them their happiness. Quite the opposite. The two had been through a lot, and if anyone deserved a happy ending, it was certainly them. But seeing them so happy and in love just reminded her that she wasn't.

"Hi, Eric." Tom shook the doctor's hand.

"Tom." Eric nodded. "Chloe and I were just talking about your victim."

"You're her doctor?"

"Yes, I was telling Chloe she's in reasonably good physical condition, especially all things considering, but psychologically? That's a totally different story."

"Think we're going to get anything out of her tonight?" Tom asked.

"I doubt it," Eric replied.

Her partner turned to her. "Maybe we just introduce ourselves, see if we can at least get confirmation that she was his victim."

Chloe had to force her brain to snap out of wallowing in her own problems and back into work mode. "Sounds like a plan."

"I'll catch you two later. Good luck with Taylor. Chloe, think about what I said." Eric shot her a serious look before walking off.

She thought Tom would pry into whatever she and Eric had been talking about, but he didn't mention it as they headed for Taylor Sallow's room. By the time they opened the door, Chloe had mostly managed to refocus on the reason for being here. It wasn't like her pain over losing her son was going anywhere, and Taylor deserved to have her one hundred percent focused.

"Ms. Sallow?" Tom began as they entered the room.

The woman in the bed shrunk away from them as though she wished she could shrink away and disappear altogether.

Tom made the introductions. "I'm Special Agent Drake, and this is my partner, Special Agent Luckman."

Learning they were law enforcement didn't seem to calm her. Taylor's green eyes darted around the room as though something might jump up and save her. It was going to take time and effort to convince this young woman that they weren't a threat to her. Taylor's breathing was quickening, and she looked like she was working herself into a panic. They needed something to calm her down, Chloe was contemplating going and getting Eric and asking him to give her something, when suddenly Taylor's eyes settled on something, and she immediately calmed.

Turning to see what had soothed the girl who had seemed to be on a quick path to hysteria, she gasped when she saw who was standing there.

"Fin," she mumbled.

"Chloe." He looked equally shocked to see her.

"What are you doing here?"

"He saved me," Taylor answered from the bed.

Saved her? How had her ex-boyfriend saved this woman? What was going on here? How had Fin ended up getting himself mixed up in her latest case? And why did being this close to him still hurt so badly?

* * * * *

10:59 P.M.

Why did it have to be Chloe working Taylor's case?

Why did he feel comforted by the fact that she looked as unhappy as he felt?

Why did he want nothing more than to pull her into his arms, kiss her senseless, then pick her up and take her home to bed?

Fin didn't know the answer to any of those questions.

Okay, that was a big fat lie. He knew the answers. He wanted to forget the last seven months had happened. He wanted to go back in time and make it so the car accident never happened and their son had been born a happy, healthy baby boy. He wanted to forget that Chloe had broken his heart when she'd packed up her stuff and walked out the door.

That was her choice. He didn't have to like it—and he didn't—but he had to accept it. She had made her choice; now they both had to live with the consequences. So why did she look so sad? She'd gotten what she'd wanted.

"You saved her?" Tom Drake asked, breaking the stifling tension that had settled in the room.

He knew Chloe's partner reasonably well, but they weren't what he'd call friends. However, right now Tom was shooting him a sympathetic look. It was a year to the day since Tom and Hannah had been thrown back together three years after they had divorced because of a crime. It had led to them reconnecting and reconciling. They'd gotten their happily ever after, but Fin didn't foresee that happening with him and Chloe. Tom and Hannah had been ripped apart because of a tragedy; they hadn't split up because they stopped loving each other.

Chloe had chosen to walk away from him.

The only explanation he could give for that was that she'd done it because she no longer wanted to be with him.

Their relationship was over.

She had left him at the lowest point in his life.

She'd left him alone, and he was furious with her for it.

He wanted to hate her; it made things so much easier.

Hating her was much harder when she was standing in front of him looking even more beautiful than he remembered. All of this would be a whole lot easier if he didn't still love her.

But what good was love when the other person turned their back on you like you meant nothing to them?

Love was nothing more than a shortcut to pain.

He'd loved his unborn son, and the child had died.

He'd loved Chloe, and she had thrown him away.

At least he had found out earlier rather than later that she didn't really love him. It would've been so much worse to find out after they'd spent years married with children.

He might still be hopelessly in love with her, but she'd made it clear it was over between them, and maybe she was right. Maybe they were never meant to be. Maybe breaking up had been for the best.

"Fin?" Tom prompted. "How did you save her?"

Right, this wasn't about him and Chloe. They were in the same room only by some fluke. This was about the traumatized young woman in the hospital bed. "I didn't really save her," he replied. "I was coming home from work, and I saw her in the street. At first, I thought she was drunk and assumed she would stumble into whichever house she'd come from. But when she headed for my house, I realized something was wrong."

"Taylor." Tom walked toward the bed. "Do you know where you were running from?"

She didn't answer, just shrank deeper into the mattress.

"Did she say anything to you?" Tom turned and asked him.

"Not much. She was freaking out until I told her I was a doctor. She told me her name, that her leg was hurt, and that she hit someone and ran."

Returning his attention to the woman in the bed, Tom asked, "Taylor, do you know the man who hurt you?"

Taylor pulled the blankets tighter around herself.

"Thanks, Fin, for helping her, but maybe it would be best if you left now," Tom said gently.

He nodded. He was more than happy to leave Taylor in the care of Eric Abbott, and Tom and Chloe. He'd done his part, he'd done the right thing, now he could go home and resume his wallowing in self-pity about the horrible year he'd had and everything that he had lost.

"You're leaving?" Taylor asked as he headed for the door.

"Tom and Chloe will look after you," he assured her.

That didn't seem to help. "You can't leave," she insisted, sitting bolt upright.

The panic in Taylor's face at the prospect was clear. She had already made him her safety net. It'd been a mistake to bring her to the hospital himself. He should have taken her inside and called an ambulance. Now she was too attached, it was going to make it that much harder for her when he left.

But he *had* to leave.

He couldn't be what Taylor needed. She needed her family and friends. She needed someone who could be there for her indefinitely. She needed someone she could count on.

Fin couldn't be any of those things for her.

He wasn't in a place in his life where he could help someone who had been through something so traumatic. He didn't know how to help her. He hadn't even been able to help his own girlfriend deal with the grief of losing their child, how on earth was he going to help Taylor deal with whatever had happened to her?

He should go now.

Drawing it out was only going to make it worse for both of them.

"You'll be fine," he said, trying to sound confident.

Tears welled up in her eyes. "Please stay with me. Just a little longer. My parents have to fly in; they won't be here for a couple of days. Can't you just stay with me until then?"

He wanted to say yes.

He was sure it was a bad idea, but how could he walk away when she begged him to be here for her? She looked so small and vulnerable curled up in the big hospital bed. Her face was so haunted. She'd been hurt by who knew what kind of monster, she'd had who knew what done to her, she was scared of being alone, and she just needed some support until her family got here.

How could he say no to that?

Spending time around Chloe was going to be hard. Although, by the way she was just standing there refusing to look at him, maybe it wouldn't be so hard after all. If they just ignored each other, then how bad could things be? And if Taylor's family would be here soon, then surely, he could spend a couple of days around his ex for such a good cause.

If it was okay with Tom and Chloe, he would stay and support Taylor. He looked at Tom, seeking his permission. When Tom nodded, he turned back to Taylor. "Okay, I'll stay with you until your family gets here."

Relief washed over her face, and she relaxed back against her pillows. "Thank you." The look of sheer gratitude in her face shook him. It had been a long time since anyone had looked at him that way.

"Taylor, can you tell us what happened to you?" Chloe asked, deliberately giving him the cold shoulder as she walked past him to the bed.

The young woman was looking exhausted. This was too much for her right now. She needed rest, she needed time to process that she was safe now and that the man who'd hurt her could never lay a hand on her again.

"I think that's enough for tonight," he announced, moving to stand protectively between Taylor and the agents.

Chloe frowned at him. "We need to know who hurt her, so we can stop him."

"I know that," he said quietly. "But upsetting her more isn't going to help you achieve that."

"You're not her doctor," Chloe retorted.

"But I am *a* doctor, and I know what she needs. You can interview her in the morning. At least give her tonight to get some sleep and adjust, then you'll get more out of her." Fin wasn't going to let his ex push him around, especially around his new charge.

"That's fine," Tom stepped in to smooth things over. "We just need to know one thing."

Fin nodded. One question was acceptable.

"Taylor, do you know who the man was that took you?" Tom asked.

The young woman looked from Tom to Fin, her eyes seeking reassurance. When he gave her an encouraging smile, she took a deep breath. "I don't know his real name."

"But ..." Chloe said when they all sensed she wasn't done.

"But he called himself The Breaker," Taylor finished.

He just managed to contain a gasp. Neither Tom nor Chloe looked surprised. They'd both known the answer Taylor would give but needed to hear her confirm it. The Breaker was a particularly vicious serial killer who already had two victims under his belt. How had Taylor managed to escape from him?

DECEMBER 19TH

7:56 A.M.

She swirled the coffee in the takeout cup she held in her hand. Chloe was so confused. Seeing Fin last night had been unexpected, but surprisingly, in a good way. She had missed him so much.

Chloe thought last night was a sign.

Exactly a year ago, Tom had walked into a crime scene and found Hannah. Despite everything that had grown between them and kept them apart, just the act of being thrown back together had been enough for them to realize that being away from each other didn't make either of them happy.

If it hadn't been for the robbery at Hannah's jewelry store, she and Tom would never have reconciled. They wouldn't be back together. They wouldn't have remarried. They wouldn't be happily living out the rest of their lives together.

That case was that one thing that had changed everything.

So what were the odds that a year to the day that her partner got his second chance she would run into her ex because of a case?

Those odds had to be astronomical.

This was it.

Her second chance. Hers and Fin's. Maybe they could find a way to sort things out just like Tom and Hannah had.

Sure, what had broken them up was very different than what had led to the destruction of Tom and Hannah's first marriage, but in the end, they'd both been ripped apart by trauma, and if her partner could fix his broken relationship, then why couldn't she?

"Chlo-ee." She blinked. "Oh, Tom."

"I've been calling your name for a solid minute, what are you so deep in thought about?"

Chloe didn't want to get into that right now. "Nothing important, just daydreaming." Fin had filled her dreams all night; if she really had been daydreaming, then she guessed he'd fill those too.

Tom arched a brow. From the look in his eyes, he clearly knew what she'd been thinking about, but he didn't push the topic. "You're wearing the reindeer beanie."

She was. She had a serious addiction to all things tacky, ugly, Christmassy clothing. She had more sweaters, pajamas, socks, scarves, onesies than was normal, and her favorite was the reindeer beanie that had been a gift from her grandmother when she was twelve—the last Christmas her grandmother had been alive. She wore it all winter long, from October first to the end of April, every single day, without fail, whether the weather was warm or freezing cold.

But this year had been different.

She'd lost her son and the man she loved, and she just hadn't been able to summon her usual joy around the holidays. What good were reindeer beanies and snowmen onesies and sweaters with Santas when she was grieving and sad and alone? Christmas was supposed to be a time to cherish the ones you loved—if you didn't have those people anymore, then Christmas lost its joy.

It wasn't until last night when she'd seen Fin that she'd felt a little flicker of hope ignite inside her.

Maybe it wasn't too late to save her relationship. She and Fin could talk. They could sort things out. She could apologize for walking away, and she could explain why she'd had to leave. Then they could get back together and everything would be okay again.

It felt like time to wear the beanie again. "It's only a week until Christmas," she told her partner in preference to explaining about her and Fin and her reconciliation hopes.

Again, it was clearly written on her partner's face that he already knew what thoughts were running through her head. Tom had really mellowed a lot since he remarried Hannah. He was still the meticulous agent who paid attention to every minute detail, but he was more easygoing now, more relaxed than when she had first met him.

Chloe was ready to put away thoughts of Fin for the time being though. They had a case to work and it was the biggest of her career so far.

"It was him. But how did she get away from him?" she wondered aloud. From what they knew about the killer, she couldn't imagine how Taylor Sallow had managed to escape.

"Hopefully Taylor can tell us that when we speak to her later today. She's had a night to get some sleep, so hopefully, we'll get more out of her than we did last night."

"Do we know how many breaks?" she asked.

"Not yet. He had her for nearly nineteen months—plenty of time to do several breaks."

She shuddered.

This killer was particularly vicious.

He'd been nicknamed The Breaker because he destroyed the homes of his victims when he abducted them. He broke every mirror, every vase, every figurine, every window in the house. Then he grabbed the woman and disappeared.

Without a trace.

There was no physical evidence left behind. There were no witnesses. There was nothing that told them who he was or where he took the women. They were just there one day and gone the next.

"Kelly Mitchell was gone for almost four years," Tom said. "There were no leads. The case went cold quickly because the cops didn't know which direction to look. There was no husband or boyfriend. There were no exes. There were no problems with friends or colleagues or neighbors. Everyone loved her, and no one had any ideas who would have taken her. The cops went through every sexual predator in the area. They searched through Kelly's life with a fine-tooth comb looking for some secret that might have gotten her killed, and they came up empty. Eventually, there was nowhere else to look, and the case was put on the back burner."

"Until her body was found at a bus stop four years later." Chloe didn't like to think about those four years and what Kelly Mitchell had suffered. She couldn't imagine what the woman's life had been like. She didn't *want* to imagine what the woman's life had been like.

"With thirty bones broken, all in various stages of healing," Tom added.

"According to the ME's report, some of the breaks looked like they'd been done four years prior to her death. Most likely, he did them one at a time. He wanted her to suffer. He enjoyed it. If he didn't, he would have just killed her and been done with it. But he didn't. He broke each bone individually and then let them heal before moving on to the next one."

What kind of sick monster did that to another human being?

Chloe had known since she was ten that monsters existed, and she had always known when she'd chosen this job that she would encounter them. But knowing that and actually working a case where she was hunting one made it so much more real.

"Within days of Kelly Mitchell's body being discovered, he'd taken another woman, Christie Neil. The cases were linked because of the women's houses. Both had been trashed in identical fashion."

"He had her for almost seven years; she had over ninety bones that had been broken by the time he killed her and dumped her," Chloe said.

"No one saw anything when he dumped the bodies. He's like a ghost. No one ever sees him come or go." Tom sounded frustrated, and she couldn't blame him. How were they going to catch this guy when they had nothing to go on? He wasn't going to stop; they both knew that. He was just going to keep snatching women and torturing and killing them. Death or arrest. Those were the only two things that would end this.

"What do you think he's trying to achieve?" she asked.

Tom arched a brow at her. "He wants to break all their bones," he said simply.

In the back of her mind, she knew that; she just didn't want to accept it. It was the only thing that made sense. He was breaking their bodies bone by bone. He broke over three times the number of bones in Christie's body than he had in Kelly's. He had improved, but in the end, he had killed them the same way.

Both Kelly and Christie had died from complications to broken bones in their spinal cord. The medical examiner said in the reports that complications from nerve and blood vessel damage had likely caused cardiac arrest.

For some insane reason, this killer seemed to want to attempt to break every bone in his victims' bodies, presumably ending with—if everything went according to his plan—their C1 and C2 neck bones.

This was so crazy, it didn't seem real.

Chloe just couldn't comprehend why anyone would want to do this to someone. "Who exactly are we looking for? This guy isn't young; it's been thirteen years since he abducted his first victim."

"That we know of," Tom inserted.

She nodded. That was true; there could have been other victims before Kelly Mitchell that they didn't know about. "He doesn't seem to care about physical appearance. All his victims have different physical characteristics. But he obviously likes younger women—they were all late teens or early twenties when he took them."

"And pretty."

"Pretty, young, and despite the interest in broken bones, neither Kelly, Christie, or Taylor had ever had a broken bone before he took them."

"Maybe that's important to him. He likes to work on a blank canvas," Tom suggested.

"No signs of sexual assault despite how long he had them."

"He doesn't need to rape them; he already has the power. He has them locked up and injured. Breaking their bones is all the high he needs."

She agreed. "So, assuming that he was at least in his early twenties when he took Kelly, he has to be mid-thirties now."

"I think he's older." Her partner looked thoughtful. "He had to be able to break each bone and make sure the women didn't die too soon."

She quickly caught on to where he was going. "He had to tend to them. You think he has some sort of medical knowledge."

Tom nodded. "I think he's more likely late thirties or early forties. He's smart, he's methodical, and he isn't reckless. He can keep his victims alive for years without rushing and losing control and killing them."

Feeling helpless, she asked, "How are we going to catch him?"

"He messed up. Somehow, he let Taylor escape. Now we have a witness. We just have to hope she knows enough to lead us straight to him."

Her partner was right. But Chloe knew her biggest struggle was going to be keeping her attention focused on Taylor and not getting distracted by Fin. Kelly Mitchell, Christie Neil, and Taylor all deserved justice, and she was determined to get it for them.

* * * * *

8:42 A.M.

She was so tired. So why couldn't she fall asleep?

Taylor had thought that the minute her head hit a pillow, she would be out. She hadn't gotten a full night's sleep in nineteen months. What sleep she had gotten hadn't been good or restful. It had been fitful, full of bad dreams, with part of her brain always remaining vigilant for any signs that the man was coming into her room.

It was hard to accept that she was safe now.

That she was away from him and there was no way he could get to her.

It didn't seem real.

She kept expecting that at any second he was going to come barging through the door like he had so many times before.

What if he did?

Supposedly there was a cop stationed at her hospital room door, but at the moment that wasn't particularly reassuring.

The cops didn't know him.

They didn't know what he was like.

They didn't know how devious he was or how smart or how cruel. It was really hard not to believe that he wouldn't come back.

That fear hadn't let go of her since she'd gone running for freedom. Now she was starting to wonder if it ever would. Maybe she would always fear that he'd come back for her. And what if the cops never found him? How could she ever be able to move on if he was still out there?

The simple answer was she wouldn't.

Even if they did find him, and he was arrested and sent to prison, there would always be the possibility that he could get out.

There was only one thing that would make her truly safe.

One thing that would ensure he could never come after her again.

He had to die.

But how?

It wasn't like she knew how to track him down. And even if she did, could she really kill him in cold blood?

After everything he'd done to her, Taylor believed that she

could. It might be the only way that she could ever have a life. She was only twenty-two. She wanted to go back and finish college. She wanted to date and fall in love and get married. She wanted to have kids and grow old and have grandchildren to spoil. She wanted a life.

"Taylor, are you sure you don't want me to give you something to help you sleep?"

A small smile danced across her lips.

Fin.

Dr. Fin Patrick.

She had really lucked out when of all the people she could have stumbled into, it had been a doctor. A *good* doctor. A pretty dreamy doctor, too.

Fin had hair as black as night and eyes the color of a summer sky. He had dimples when he smiled—which he rarely did—and looked like he was in his late twenties.

As hot as she thought the doctor was, that wasn't what she cared about.

He had saved her.

If he hadn't stopped to help her, then she would have either collapsed and been left at the mercy of the elements, or she would have wandered into a road and been hit by a car.

Instead, Fin had come to her rescue.

He was her hero.

He made her feel safe, and when he looked at her, he made her feel warm. It was weird, but when she looked into his eyes, a warmth washed over her, like his eyes had transported her to some tropical island and she was staring at the endless blue sky and the deep blue ocean while the sun shone down upon her.

"Taylor, I know you're awake. You've been awake all night."

Fin knew that because he had stayed by her bedside.

Last night when he'd said he was leaving, she'd thought she would lose it. How could he leave her? What would she do without him? She would be all alone. The very idea of being alone again was terrifying. She'd been alone for nineteen long months with no one to help her or support her—no one to stop that horrible man from hurting her.

Now she had Fin.

She *needed* him.

Surely, he could see that.

Even once her parents got back, she would need him. Her parents had never made her feel warm inside like Fin did. They'd had her and her brother when they were in their late forties, and as older parents, they'd given their children everything they ever wanted. Except their time. They'd always been too busy to do things with her and bought her off to make up for it. Taylor loved them, but she didn't feel close to them. They'd never developed that parent-daughter bond.

But she already felt that bond with Fin.

Her knight in shining armor was everything she could ever hope for in a man.

She didn't want him to leave her side.

Ever.

Slowly, she blinked open her eyes to find him standing beside her bed, looking down at her. He was tall; she liked that in a man. At almost five foot ten, she towered over most women and quite a few men, so a man who was taller than her was always on her list. She bet he had muscles to die for under his plain gray sweater.

The color of his sweater complemented his eyes, made them seem even bluer, and she lost herself staring into them.

"Taylor?"

She forced herself to focus. Lack of sleep and her jumbled thoughts made it hard, but she managed to look at him. "Yeah?"

"You should eat something."

"Not hungry." Even the thought of food made her nauseous.

Fin frowned. "Your body needs fuel. It also needs sleep," he said rebukingly.

"I tried. I just can't," she said helplessly. She didn't know how to explain everything she was thinking and feeling right now. She barely comprehended it herself, let alone trying to untangle it enough to explain it to someone else.

He gave her a long assessing look. A doctor look. The kind of look that seemed to see right inside her and decipher everything, then stow it away for future reference. "Tom and Chloe will be coming to talk to you soon," he announced.

Panic sliced through her.

She wanted to say no. She didn't want to see them.

But if she didn't see them and talk to them and tell them what she knew, then how could they find him?

And if they didn't find him, how could she really be free?

She was so confused.

This was all too much. Being free was so much more complicated than she had thought it would be. When she was being held captive, she would daydream about being rescued and returning to live in the real world. In every single one of those daydreams, everything had gone so smoothly. It was like the second she was out of that room, everything returned to normal. She felt good; she was happy and whole. She didn't feel like she was broken inside with no idea how—or even if—it was possible to put all the pieces of herself back together again.

Reality wasn't like her dreams had been.

Reality was messy and dark and confusing.

Reality was filled with questions that had no answers, pain that had no balm, and fears that had nothing to quash them.

Reality sucked.

She wanted her life to go back to what it had been before. She didn't want the last nineteen months and the things that man had done to her to mar her. She didn't want scars— physical or psychological. She didn't want to be affected; she didn't want to be traumatized; she didn't want to be a victim.

"Taylor?" Fin reached out and took her hand.

His touch anchored her.

As long as Fin was here, she could do this.

"You won't leave me, right?"

"I think they would prefer to interview you without me being present," he said gently.

"No," she practically shouted, surprised by the strength and conviction in her tone. "I can't do the interview unless you're there with me. I can't."

She needed him to understand that.

She needed him to understand how important he was to her.

"Don't leave me, please. You promised you wouldn't." Taylor deliberately left out that he had promised to stay with her only until her family got here.

He smiled. A breathtakingly beautiful smile. "Don't worry. I'm not going anywhere. I promised I would be here for you. If Tom and Chloe have a problem with my being here while they speak with you, then they'll just have to get over it."

Relief settled over her.

Fin was staying, and she didn't care whether those FBI agents didn't like it. She didn't like them. Especially the woman. There was something between Fin and the woman, and she didn't want anything or any*one* getting between her and Fin.

If Taylor had her way, Dr. Fin Patrick would never leave her side again for as long as she lived.

* * * * *

9:09 A.M.

Fin was starting to think it was a bad idea agreeing to stay with Taylor until her parents arrived.

She was getting too attached.

Way too attached.

He'd been trying to do the right thing, but now he thought he might actually be making things worse. She needed stability, and that was something he couldn't give her. He could be here to support her and keep her company while she waited for her family to arrive, but then he was leaving. He already knew that wasn't going to go well.

Taylor wanted him to be at her side permanently.

But that was never going to happen.

He wanted Chloe and Tom to find who had hurt her. He wanted her to be safe and to heal and to be able to move on with her life. But he wasn't a part of her life, and he wasn't ever going to be.

Despite what she thought, he wasn't what she needed.

She needed the people who loved her and cared about her.

Fin understood why she had latched on to him; in her mind, he was her savior, her white knight, her hero. But in time, once she started to heal, she would realize that her feelings were getting jumbled up. Gratitude over him helping her—really doing no more than any decent human being would do—didn't mean love.

He really hoped this didn't turn out to be a huge mistake. He didn't want to end up causing Taylor more harm than good.

"What if I can't tell them what they want to know?" Taylor asked quietly, looking up at him with all the vulnerability and fragility of a distressed child.

"Why would you think that?" he asked.

Before Taylor could answer, the door to her hospital room swung open and Chloe and Tom walked in.

Chloe's eyes grew wide when she saw him, and something flittered quickly through them before it was gone and she frowned at him. Apparently, she was as unhappy about the prospect of having to spend time around him as he was about having to spend time around her.

"You're here," Chloe said, stating the blatantly obvious.

"I told Taylor I was here to support her until her family arrived." He raised a challenging brow. Part of him wanted her to try to stop him, to make him leave. Fin wanted an excuse to unleash the anger he'd been bottling up inside ever since she'd packed her things and walked out the door.

She looked like she was going to argue, but before she could, Taylor said, "If he doesn't stay, I can't talk to you. I need him here."

"That's fine." Tom smiled and crossed the room, pulling up a seat and sitting beside the bed. "How are you feeling, Taylor?"

"I'm okay," Taylor replied warily. It was clear she didn't trust anyone but him right now.

"We spoke with Dr. Abbott. He says you should be able to go home tomorrow," Tom continued, seemingly undaunted by Taylor's hostility.

Since she still held his hand, Fin felt the small shiver that rippled through her. They hadn't discussed it—they hadn't really spoken much at all—but he knew the prospect of leaving the hospital scared her. Being here offered some measure of safety and stability, but once she left, she had to reenter the real world. And that was going to be a lot harder to do with the man who had abducted her still on the loose.

"Taylor, before you were taken, do you remember anything unusual happening, or anyone suspicious hanging around?" Chloe asked, jumping straight into the interrogation.

With her gaze fixed firmly on Tom, she said, "There was something."

"What was it?" Tom asked.

"There was a car. I thought it might be following me," Taylor said hesitantly.

"Thought?" Chloe echoed.

Again, Taylor focused on Tom—it seemed she didn't like Chloe. Perhaps she saw her as some sort of threat. She couldn't be more wrong. Chloe wasn't the least bit interested in him. "I thought I was probably just being paranoid. Who would be following me?"

"Did you tell anyone?" Tom asked.

Taylor shook her head. "I thought it was just my imagination, but then …"

"Then what, Taylor?" Tom prompted gently.

"Then I thought someone might have been inside my house."

"What made you think that?" Tom asked. It seemed he and Chloe had somehow decided without discussing it that Taylor responded better to him, so he would lead the questioning.

"It was silly," Taylor hedged.

"Nothing you thought was silly. Anything, no matter how small, could be important," Tom assured her.

"A vase was broken. It could have just been my cat," Taylor added quickly.

Immediately, Fin knew that it wasn't the cat. He knew who The Breaker was and what he did. Taylor had said that was what the man who'd held her captive for nineteen months had called himself. Maybe if Taylor had realized the significance of the broken vase, she might have reported it and possibly even have avoided being the serial killer's next victim.

"But you don't think so," Tom said.

Slowly, Taylor shook her head.

"Why?"

"Because the vase was downstairs in my lounge room and I usually kept the cat upstairs during the day because otherwise, she used to love to rip my couches."

"You didn't report the break-in."

"I couldn't. It was the day he took me. I got home late from work; I saw the vase, I cleaned it up. I heated a frozen meal for dinner, ate it, then studied for a test I had the next day. Then I went upstairs to start getting ready for bed and went to take a shower."

"What do you remember about the abduction itself?" Tom asked.

"Not a lot. I went upstairs, turned the shower on, then while the water was heating, I stripped off my clothes, put them in the hamper, then got in. I was just rinsing the shampoo out of my hair when I felt a prick in my leg. I instantly felt dizzy, my limbs went numb, and my vision went all fuzzy. Then I passed out." Taylor paused, looking lost in thought. "He was in there the whole time, wasn't he?"

Even Fin knew the answer to that.

The killer had broken in, smashed the vase, then hid and waited for Taylor to come home. As soon as he knew she was distracted and wouldn't notice him coming or attempt to get away from him, he had struck.

"He probably was," Tom said gently. Having eased Taylor into the interview slowly, the agent moved on to the harder questions. "Where were you when you woke up?"

Taylor drew in a long, shaky breath. Her hand squeezed his painfully tightly, but he didn't pull away, just squeezed back, very aware of the fact that Chloe was watching his every move like a hawk. Fin didn't really know why she was suddenly so interested in him. It had been five months since she left, and in that time, she hadn't contacted him once. Now, all of a sudden, she didn't like another woman holding his hand? Well, that was too bad. She lost the right to care about who he spent time with when she dumped him and walked out the door.

"I was in a tiny room. Lying on a bed. There was a toilet, a small tub with a shower head attached to the wall beside it, a table with two chairs, and a weird looking bench type thing with a whole bunch of leather straps attached to it," Taylor explained in a rush.

"Were you restrained?"

"No. I was just laid out on the bed wearing a dress like the one I was wearing when I ran."

"Had he sexually assaulted you?" Tom asked tightly. Fin noticed the tremor in his jaw. Sexual assault was a sensitive topic for Tom, given what had happened to Hannah.

Taylor shook her head.

"You said that the man who took you called himself The Breaker, but do you know what his real name is?"

She tensed, and Fin assumed this was the cause of her fear that she couldn't tell the agents what they wanted to know.

"Taylor?" Tom prompted.

"Just tell them what you can," Fin told her, patting her shoulder with his free hand.

She drew in another deep breath. "I'm sorry. I don't know his name. I'm sorry," she said again. Her posture had gone defensive, and she sounded afraid, as though she wasn't altogether sure that Tom and Chloe wouldn't punish her for not giving them the correct answer. The Breaker hadn't kept her restrained, so he'd obviously had to use something else to keep her in line, no doubt threats. "I'm so sorry," Taylor continued to babble, ignoring Tom when he tried to reassure her. "How can you find him when I don't know his name?" She was crying now, quickly growing hysterical. "I'm sorry, I'm sorry," she continued to repeat the words like a chant as she threw herself into his arms.

"I'll go get Dr. Abbott," Tom announced, hurrying out of the room.

Chloe didn't move.

Her gaze fixed firmly on him.

Fin felt odd holding another woman in his arms. Almost like he was cheating.

But he wasn't.

Chloe had ended their relationship.

So why was she looking at him like she still cared?

* * * * *

5:16 P.M.

Why did she want to work with little kids again?

Right now, Avery couldn't remember why the idea had ever

been appealing.

She was exhausted. Ten hours with twenty three-year-olds and she felt like she needed to take the longest, hottest bubble bath, and then fall into bed and sleep for a day.

Too bad she couldn't.

She had to be back at work at seven o'clock tomorrow morning.

Why did she do this to herself?

Avery set down her bag on the table by her apartment door and pulled out her cell. A sheet of paper came with it; on it was a brightly colored drawing of her that one of the little kids had done at day care today. Flowers and butterflies and big fat yellow and black bumblebees filled up almost every available bit of space.

She smiled.

This was why she did this.

Working with children was what she had wanted to do for as long as she could remember. Pictures like this made the exhaustion more than worth it.

Taking the picture with her, she went to the kitchen and hung it up on her fridge. She was going to have to start hanging artwork the kids made for her someplace else, the refrigerator was almost full now; a colorful patchwork of crayon drawings and finger paintings and crafts.

The children were so sweet, she loved her days at the day care center. She couldn't wait until she graduated with her degree and could go to work full time. Working with kids gave her life some meaning. It gave her a purpose. It made her feel like she was contributing something to the world.

Sticking the picture into the last spare bit of space, Avery stuck a couple of pieces of bread into the toaster. It wasn't much of a dinner, but she was too tired to cook something, and if she ate a quick meal, then she might be able to stay awake long enough to call her boyfriend after her bath.

Not bothering to butter her toast when it popped up, she

merely picked it up and took it with her down the hall to her bedroom, kicking off her shoes as she went. Avery loved to walk barefoot—if she had her way, she'd never wear shoes again. Although, that wouldn't be very practical for the cold, snowy winters. Still, whenever she was indoors, her shoes came off.

In the bedroom, she froze.

The vase of flowers her boyfriend had given her for their six-month anniversary was laying on the floor beside her bed. The crystal vase was shattered into a million pieces.

How had that happened?

Avery looked at the window, but it was closed, just how she'd left it. She didn't have any pets that could have knocked it over.

Confused, she set down the half-eaten piece of toast on the dresser and went and gathered the roses up. They were still wet like the vase had been knocked over recently. She shook them off and carried them back to the kitchen, retrieving another vase and filling it with water, and then putting the flowers inside. Leaving them on the counter, Avery grabbed a brush and dustpan and returned to the bedroom.

It was so weird. How did the flowers end up on the ground?

Had someone broken in here?

Nervously, she looked about.

It *didn't* look like anyone was in here with her, nor did it appear anyone had been in here earlier. Nothing looked out of place, and it didn't look like anything was missing.

Then it hit her.

Her mom.

Her mother was the ultimate control freak. She had micromanaged every single aspect of Avery's life since she was born. She was nineteen now, an adult, but still, her mom couldn't let go. She disapproved of every relationship she'd ever had and disliked her current boyfriend because she believed that he wasn't good enough. Avery still lived on her parents' property, in a small guesthouse apartment out the back. It wasn't that she wanted to, but her parents were paying for her college, and one of the conditions was that she still lived at home. This guesthouse had been the compromise.

She and her boyfriend had talked about the possibility of her taking out student loans to pay for her own education. Between the two of them, they could probably make it work. He was a few years older than her and had already graduated. He had a good job, and between his wages and her continuing to work a couple of days a week at the day care, then they might just be able to manage.

Besides, anything had to be better than this.

Avery wasn't sure she could take it any longer.

Especially if her mom had taken to breaking in and snooping around.

Annoyed now, she began to gather up the broken crystal shards. How dare her mom think it was okay to come in here uninvited while she was at work. This kind of behavior had to stop. If her mom continued to act this way, then it was going to wind up ruining their relationship, and Avery did *not* want that.

She loved her mother, despite her control freak tendencies. She wanted them to be close; she wanted her mom to be an active part of her life, especially once she was married and had kids of her own. But if her mother was always treating her like a helpless child, how could that happen?

It was time for her to move out.

This settled things.

She'd take her bath and then she'd call her boyfriend, and they'd formulate a plan. He'd already asked her to move in with him, so Avery knew he'd be excited to hear she was ready to move off her parents' property. Then she would have to apply for loans, which might mean missing the rest of this semester, but at least she'd be able to pick up more days at work. More work meant more money.

Tomorrow she would have to talk to her mother.

She didn't relish the idea, but if she wanted to be treated like an adult then she had to act like an adult, and adults didn't run and hide from their problems, they faced them and dealt with them.

And her parents would understand.

She was sure of it because, underneath her controlling behaviors, her mother loved her.

Besides, it was Christmastime, and that was the season for joy and peace and goodwill toward men.

Everything would be fine.

"Ooh," she squeaked as she scooped up the last of the crystal and a shard sliced through the palm of her hand. A spot of blood bloomed and then oozed out, trickling slowly down toward her wrist.

Sighing, Avery brought the dustpan with her to the bathroom and emptied it into the wastebasket, then held her hand under the running faucet. This was *not* how she had envisioned her evening turning out. Maybe she should skip the bath, make a quick call to her boyfriend and arrange to talk to him in the morning, then go straight to bed.

It was tempting, but nothing was going to relax her like a steaming hot bubble bath. If she went to bed now, she probably wasn't going to be able to fall asleep. She'd just lie there running through her head what she was going to say to her boyfriend and then her mom.

Bath, it was.

Turning off the tap, she tossed some bath salts and bubble bath into the tub, then turned the hot water on full. Her hand seemed to have stopped bleeding, so she pulled out a band-aid from the first aid kit she kept under her bathroom sink and taped it over the small cut.

Already the steam filling the room was calming her. Avery felt herself relax bit by bit, her worries and anxieties fading away. Slipping out of her clothes, she dumped them in the hamper, then twisted her hair up into a bun on the top of her head to keep it out of the water. She wasn't in the mood to wash her long, dark hair, and if it got wet, it would be a fizzy mess tomorrow.

Avery added a little bit of cold water to the bath, then climbed in. As soon as she sunk down into the bubbly heat, her muscles loosened up, and her mind cleared. This was pure heaven. Baths were like magic. They possessed the power to wipe everything away and help her come at things from a new, calmer, clearer perspective.

She'd find a way to make everything work. Who knows, maybe her mom would even be proud of her for wanting to take responsibility for her own life and make her own way.

Closing her eyes, she sank down deeper until the water came right up to her chin. Her eyes drifted closed. She was so tired, and the stress of finding out her mom had been rummaging through her house had just pushed her over the edge. A quick nap sounded pretty good right about now.

She was just drifting off when something sharp pricked her shoulder.

Startled, she sloshed water all over the side of the bath as she bolted upright.

Had a spider just bitten her?

Avery had a major phobia of the disgusting eight-legged creatures.

Her body started to tingle, her limbs quickly going numb. Her eyesight began to fade, and there was a rushing sound in her ears.

Then the world was swallowed up by darkness.

* * * * *

9:58 P.M.

This was probably a terrible idea.

Chloe knew that and yet her feet kept walking forward.

She didn't even know if Fin was on the same page as her.

Strike that—she didn't even know what page *she* was on.

All she knew was that something was drawing her back toward Fin like some long piece of invisible string. All day she hadn't been able to get him out of her mind. By the time she and Tom had called it a night and gone their separate ways, her partner had been getting annoyed with her constant zoning out.

She was going to have to get that under control.

Whatever this confusing thing was that she felt for Fin, she had to keep her mind on her job. If The Breaker stuck to his regular pattern, then he would be taking another girl to replace Taylor soon. Or he would be coming back for Taylor. Either way, the man was dangerous and needed to be stopped, and she couldn't do that if she kept getting distracted by her ex-boyfriend.

Maybe it would help if she could figure out what exactly it was that she wanted.

Did she want to just make peace with Fin, get some closure, and move on?

Did she want to make peace and become friends?

Did she want to make peace and get back together with him?

Chloe truly wasn't sure what she wanted—she just knew that the more she tried to forget about Fin, the more she thought about him. And that had to mean something.

So, she was here at the hospital to see him. She wasn't sure yet what she was going to say to him when she saw him, and she couldn't deny she was a little daunted by the prospect of seeing him again—he certainly hadn't been particularly happy to see her earlier, but she needed to know. She needed to be able to sort out her jumbled feelings. She needed answers, and she hoped that by talking to Fin, she could get them.

She saw him up ahead, striding purposefully toward a room.

Taylor's room.

She frowned. He was really attached to the woman he'd known only twenty-four hours. The feeling seemed to be mutual. Taylor had been all over him earlier, refusing to speak with them unless

Fin stayed with her, holding his hand, throwing herself into his arms when she broke down.

Fin seemed to enjoy it.

That sparked a tiny jolt of jealousy inside her.

Was it just because she and Fin shared a past or because she wanted a future with him?

It was really annoying her that she didn't know the answer to that.

What was wrong with her? Why couldn't she figure out her own life and her own feelings? She'd never had trouble with it before. She'd always known what she wanted and gone after it, but now she felt so wishy-washy and confused. Like someone had tossed her into a blender with a whole mishmash of emotions and left her to try to make sense of them while they were all being thrown about.

She really hated feeling this way.

And it was time to make it stop.

She was regaining control of her life. Losing her baby had really shaken her in a way that she would never fully recover from, but it was time to take charge. If she wanted something, she had to work for it. Now it was time to find out if she and Fin could possibly reclaim what they'd had or if things were over between them for good.

Determinedly, Chloe strode toward Taylor's room.

Her confidence faltered a little as her hands landed on the door, and she had pushed it open barely a millimeter when she heard voices.

"You're back." Taylor sounded excited.

"I said I'd pop in after my shift," Fin replied.

Chloe knew she shouldn't eavesdrop. She should either keep moving forward and go in and ask to speak to Fin, or she should retreat and go home with her tail between her legs and leave Fin to Taylor Sallow.

She did neither.

Instead, she stayed right where she was and continued with her spying.

"Can you stay here tonight?" Taylor asked.

Fin paused, then said, "I need to go home, check on a few things, shower, and sleep before my shift tomorrow."

He didn't sound very convincing, and apparently, Taylor thought that too, because she said, "I don't feel safe when you're not here."

"You are safe here, Taylor," Fin said. "You've been here all day while I was working and you were fine."

"That was different," Taylor insisted. "I knew you were here in the building. You were close by. But if you go home, I'll be all alone. Please, couldn't you just stay here tonight? Then tomorrow, if you have to go home, you can. Please, Fin, please."

The begging seemed to do the trick. "I suppose I could stay, just for tonight," Fin said.

Chloe shook her head. That was a mistake. The more Fin became Taylor's pillar of support, the more it would hurt her when he left.

A horrible thought struck her.

What if it wasn't just Fin trying to be a good guy and do the right thing?

What if he *wanted* to be here for Taylor?

What if he didn't intend to walk away?

The very thought sent ice flowing through her veins.

She hated the idea.

She was definitely jealous.

That had to be a good thing, she convinced herself. That meant that she still cared enough about Fin to be upset by the idea that he might be moving on.

Maybe her feelings for him had never gone away; maybe they'd just been buried.

By pain and loss and grief and guilt.

Their son's death shouldn't have pushed them apart—it should have brought them together. She and Fin had been in love. They'd wanted to spend the rest of their lives together. Losing their son shouldn't have changed that.

It shouldn't have changed anything.

And maybe it hadn't.

Maybe it had just clouded things a bit. The same way the clouds covered the sun. They made it invisible for a time, but it never disappeared. It was always there.

Just like her love for Fin.

Grief might have clouded it in the last seven months, but it was still there.

"Thank you," Taylor said inside the room. "Thank you for everything you've done for me, Fin. Without you, I don't know what I'd do."

"Eavesdropping?"

Chloe jumped a mile and nearly let out a very girly shriek. Eric Abbott stood there, a small smirk on his face. Her cheeks burned, and she quickly moved away from the door before Fin found out that she'd been listening in on his conversation with Taylor. She thought about denying what she'd been doing, but what was the point? Eric had probably been watching her hovering at the door for the last couple of minutes.

"Fin in there?" Eric asked, following after her.

"Yes."

"With Taylor?"

She rolled her eyes. "You know she's in there too."

"You don't like the idea of him being that close to another woman."

"They aren't close," she protested. "He's just helping her. She's been through hell. You know that. You know what that man does to his victims. Fin found her, and he feels responsible for her. He doesn't want her to be alone; he just wants to help her until her family gets here."

"You don't have to convince me," Eric said quietly. "Sounds

like you need to convince yourself."

He was right.

She needed to convince herself that Fin still loved her even after she broke his heart by walking away. She had to convince herself that she hadn't thrown everything away just because of guilt. She had to convince herself that not only could she heal from the loss of her baby, but that she could reclaim her life.

Coming here tonight might not have turned out the way she'd expected, but it had given her the answers that she'd sought.

Well, some of them, anyway.

Now she knew what she wanted.

She wanted Fin.

She just had to find out if he still wanted her.

Chloe was afraid it was already too late. That she'd ruined things beyond repair. She couldn't blame Fin if he didn't want to forgive her for walking away from him when they had needed each other so badly. She just needed a chance to explain everything to him. To explain why she'd needed time and space.

The only problem was, she wasn't sure exactly what that explanation would be.

Maybe there was a way to figure out the answers she needed. To figure herself out. She'd thought it was something she could do alone. Something that would sort itself out if only she gave it enough time.

She was strong, independent, and used to doing things herself.

But sometimes, that wasn't possible.

Sometimes, you needed a little help.

"Eric, can I have your brother's number?"

* * * * *

11:11 P.M.

He watched with eager anticipation.

Surely, it couldn't be much longer before the girl woke up.

Avery Ormont was a little bigger than he'd realized. He liked his women small, fragile, vulnerable, helpless, and if he'd realized Avery wasn't quite as tiny as he'd thought, he would have picked someone else. She'd bulked up a bit since he'd last seen her. She must have been working out at the gym.

It wasn't that he was worried about her potentially having a little extra strength; she was still only a bit over five feet tall while he was comfortably over six feet. If it came down to a battle of physical strength, which it never would, he would easily win.

He just preferred to break little things.

He was starting to get impatient. When he'd seen that Avery was bigger than he had anticipated, he had upped the dose of tranquilizers he'd given her to knock her out. He must have over calculated and given her more than she'd needed because she had been out for a lot longer than he had expected.

Still, surely it couldn't be much longer now.

As if on cue, Avery moaned and began to stir.

This is what he lived for—to know that these beautiful, breakable girls were completely and utterly at his mercy. It was such an invigorating feeling. Nothing compared to it.

"Hello, Avery." He stood and walked closer to the bed, but not too close; the girl wasn't restrained, and he wasn't in the mood to have to physically restrain her should she try to attack him. He didn't want to have to injure her.

Yet.

He was very precise and specific about how and when he touched his girls.

Avery was waking up quickly, and she clearly knew something was wrong. She scrambled up into a sitting position, and when she caught sight of him, she shuffled backward on the bed until she was pressed into the corner.

The room was small. A bed, a toilet, a tub with a showerhead, a table with two chairs—which was where he'd been sitting—and the table where he performed his work. He had locked the door, and he had the key hidden in a pocket on the inside of his sweater. He was also armed. He wouldn't shoot her, of course; he couldn't risk destroying his work before he even began. But it was amazing how far just the threat of being shot went to convince someone to do what you told them to.

"I'm so glad you're awake." He smiled at her.

Her dark eyes assessed him, then scanned the room, trying to decide what her best option was. Should she try to fight him, or should she try to run?

Neither was a viable option.

He just hoped Avery was smart enough to come to that conclusion on her own.

It seemed she was because she didn't move. Her face fell as resignation settled over her. But her eyes. Her eyes remained alive. They blazed with anger and indignation.

A fire began to burn inside him.

This could be the *one*.

The one that actually worked.

Every time he tried this, he failed. It didn't work. He improved with each try, but it was never enough.

One day, he would, though.

One day, he'd achieve his goal.

And this could be it.

This could be the girl who helped him do it.

Excitement almost overrode his common sense, and he wanted to throw her on his table and begin his work right now, but he would have to wait. Give her a day or two to adjust. He wanted her healthy and strong; it was the only way this could work. Today he would teach her the rules and then perhaps in a day or two he would begin.

As he watched Avery, she gave the room a more detailed once-over. Her gaze settled on one particular wall, and then her eyes darted back to him, questions shouting out of them.

He smiled at her. "Do you know who I am?" he asked her.

She looked like she was going to be stubborn and petulant, like a spoiled child, and refuse to answer. But then she appeared to rethink things, no doubt believing if she did as he wanted then he might let her go. Avery gave one sharp shake of her head.

"I am The Breaker," he informed her, watching her for signs of recognition.

Her face remained blank. It didn't look like she had ever heard of him. He supposed it made sense, although it was a blow to his ego. Avery was nineteen. When he'd started on his quest thirteen years ago, she would have been only a child, most likely shielded from the worst of the world's happenings.

"Those pictures on the wall." He walked over to the ones that had captured her attention. "Belonged to the previous occupants of this room."

Fear flared on her face, and she shrank farther away from him. Avery stared at the skeleton pictures, unsure of what their relationship was to his other victims.

"See the black marks?"

She nodded.

"Those are the bones I broke." He stared at the pictures, a feeling of peace and tranquility washing over him as he reminisced. He had enjoyed his time with those girls. Kelly Mitchell, Christie Neil, Taylor Sallow—those women were a part of him now, just as he was a part of them, and he would never forget the time they had spent together.

He remembered their fear.

He remembered their screams.

He remembered their pain.

All three had been a balm to his soul. Sustenance as vital to him as food and water. He needed them to live. He had to feel their suffering to survive.

With each girl he'd gotten better, he'd gotten closer. If Taylor hadn't gotten away, then she might have been the one. But now he had a new girl, and he was sure that he could make it all the way with her. He was sure of it.

"Every time I broke one of their bones, I marked it off on here," he said, his fingers tracing lightly over the pictures.

"Why?" Avery asked softly, the terror in her voice like a rush of endorphins.

"So I could keep track."

"Of what?"

He was sure it must be obvious, but the teenager was apparently clinging desperately to denial. Still, he decided to indulge her. "Of each bone that I broke. I like to do it one at a time until I've broken every bone in their body. I haven't succeeded yet, but I think you might be the one who helps me do it."

Avery remained frozen in place for a second, then she sprang to life.

With an ear-piercing shriek, she flung herself off the bed and began to tear around the room, desperately searching for a way out.

It was a little amusing. She reminded him of a rat in a maze, searching frantically for something that was only there by the goodwill of another.

Well, he was Avery's only hope at goodwill.

Without him, she would get nothing but pain and then eventually death.

Striding over to her, he hooked an arm around her waist and yanked her up against his chest.

"That's enough of that," he said firmly. He was in charge here, and while he might tolerate a small amount of bad behavior because he knew this was all new and shocking, he wouldn't accept this kind of nonsense indefinitely.

The girl continued her wild struggles.

"Enough," he ordered loudly. "Enough."

With the last sob, Avery fell silent, her body going limp in his grip.

"I can make your time here better or worse. It's entirely up to you. If you choose to be obedient, to follow the rules, to do as I tell you, then I'll treat your wounds, set the breaks, and give you drugs for the pain. If you can't manage basic manners and obedience, then you will get nothing."

He let the threat hang in the air, and he knew it had sunk in when he felt a shudder ripple through her, then she tried gently to stand on her own two feet. He released her, and she stood, straightening her spine. He appreciated that she hadn't thrown a barrage of questions at him about why he'd taken her, and why he was doing this to her, and pleading and bargaining with him to let her go.

"There is no way out of this room." He wouldn't tell her that Taylor had indeed managed to escape. There was no need to; it wouldn't be happening again. "This is your life now. Be smart. Don't make this harder than it has to be. Go and lie down, the drugs will still be in your system for a while longer. I'll be back later with some food."

He waited to see if the girl would obey.

He was pleased when she did.

Already he knew she was going to be better than all the others.

He may have taken Avery, he may even be thrilled to have her as his, but that didn't mean he wasn't going to get Taylor Sallow back.

DECEMBER 20TH

9:33 A.M.

"He didn't wait long before taking his next victim," Chloe said as she and Tom walked up the drive of the Ormont family's property.

She'd been surprised when they'd received a phone call saying that a nineteen-year-old girl had gone missing and that it was believed she was a victim of The Breaker. The killer never waited too long between killing one girl and taking the next, but it had only been a little over twenty-four hours since Taylor Sallow had escaped, and already, he had moved on.

Chloe had been disappointed that Taylor hadn't been able to give them a name. She'd spent nineteen months with this man; it seemed like a given that she would be able to lead them straight to her abductor. But that obviously wasn't going to be the case. So far, it didn't seem like Taylor knew anything that was going to help them catch this guy, which did not bode well for Avery Ormont.

"No, he didn't," Tom agreed.

He sounded a little confused. She pulled her coat tighter wishing she'd worn a beanie. She never wore the reindeer one when she was going to a crime scene or an interview—it seemed too unprofessional—but she should have gone with something because her ears were freezing. "You thought he would make a play at getting Taylor back?" she asked her partner.

"Yes. We profiled him as a control freak and a perfectionist. That she managed to escape must be driving him crazy. I'd think he'd want to get her back."

"Maybe he does. But if he's as smart as we think he is, then he'd know that he won't be able to just walk up and take her. He'd have to know that we'd be making sure she was protected. Maybe he's going to wait a while, then when he thinks we've let our guard down, he'll try to get her back," she suggested.

"So far, he's managed to remain reasonably patient. He works methodically through breaking his victims' bones; it doesn't seem like he's rushing. But how long can that patience last?"

She didn't bother to answer her partner's rhetorical question.

They both knew the answer.

It was unlikely that his patience would last forever.

Assuming they were right and his goal was to break every bone in someone's body before killing them, then he was bound to eventually get frustrated when he kept failing.

When he got frustrated, he was likely to become even more dangerous.

And when he did, they could expect the body count to rise, and quickly.

"Hey, Savannah," she greeted her friend at the door to the small guesthouse at the back of the property where Avery lived.

Savannah Watson had been her friend for a long time. They'd gone through the FBI academy together, but before they'd graduated Savannah had been severely injured in an attempted abduction. Those injuries had left her unable to walk without the use of a cane, and thus ruined her dreams of becoming an agent. Instead, Savannah had transferred to the FBI's Evidence Response Team. They had remained friends, and Chloe loved it when they worked the same case because sometimes their busy lives interfered with them having time to hang out.

"Hi, Chlo, Tom." She gave them each a smile.

"Can we come in?" Tom asked.

Savannah nodded and handed them both booties to slip on over their shoes.

"Did you find anything?" Chloe asked.

"So far, nothing that's going to help you," Savannah replied. "Like the other scenes, all the windows and vases and mirrors were broken. I did find one vase that looked like it might have been broken by Avery herself."

They followed Savannah through the small house to the bathroom. She surveyed the place as they went. It looked like a typical teenage girl lived here. There were magazines piled up on the coffee table in the living room, an assortment of gadgets lay scattered about on various countertops. In the bathroom there was a curling wand, straightening iron, and so many items of makeup she could open a store.

The bath was filled with water, perhaps a little lower than Chloe would have expected, so she assumed that the killer had drugged Avery while she'd been in it and then dragged her out once she passed out.

"In the dustbin, I found broken pieces of a vase, and in the bedroom, there were a few drops of blood. I'm guessing she broke it, cleaned it up, then got in the bath where he took her," Savannah said.

Chloe shook her head. "The killer broke the vase."

"Before he drugged her?" Savannah asked.

"We think it's what he did with Taylor Sallow," Tom explained. "She said there was a broken vase that day. She thought someone might have broken in, but she didn't see anything missing or out of place."

"If that's true, and he did the same thing here, then it obviously didn't worry Avery enough to go up to her parents' house," Savannah said.

"Have you found anything else?" she asked. She wanted to end this case. Now. For several reasons, some of them selfish. Chloe honestly wanted to find this guy before Avery got hurt, before he could come back for Taylor, and before he went after anyone else. But she couldn't deny that part of her also wanted to find this guy because she didn't like Fin hanging around Taylor. She was jealous. And scared. She was afraid the more time he spent with Taylor, the more attached he might get. He might even start to develop feelings for her. The idea of Fin falling in love with someone else made her feel sick to her stomach. She didn't want things to be permanently over between them.

"I'm guessing he wore gloves like he did at the other abduction scenes. I'm sorry I can't be more helpful." Savannah's blue eyes looked guilty like she was personally to blame for the lack of physical evidence the killer left behind.

"Not your fault," Chloe reminded her.

"If there's anything here, I'll find it," Savannah assured them.

"I'm sure you will," Tom agreed, smiling at her.

"We should go interview the boyfriend and the parents," Chloe said to her partner. While she knew her friend would find anything that was here, they all knew there was nothing to find. Taylor had mentioned the possibility that someone might have been following her in the days leading up to her abduction; maybe Avery's family had also noticed something. That at least might give them a direction to move in.

"Good luck with that," Savannah said. When they both arched questioning brows at her, she elaborated, "They were arguing outside when I got here. I don't think the parents like the boyfriend very much."

Hopefully, that wasn't going to be a hindrance to the interviews. "I'll call you later, Sav," Chloe said as she and Tom turned to leave. She needed to talk to her friend about Fin and get Savannah's opinion on things. She wanted to know if the sudden resurgence of feelings meant anything and if she should get back together with him or if she was just lonely.

As they approached the front door of the main house, they could hear raised voices. Savannah was right. Avery's parents and her boyfriend clearly didn't get along.

Tom rolled his eyes and knocked on the door. Neither of them wanted to waste time refereeing bickering relatives. They needed information that would help them find Avery.

"Yes?" A thin woman in her forties, with dark hair pulled up into a tight bun, accentuating her angular face, threw open the door and practically glared at them.

"Mrs. Ormont?" Tom asked.

"Yes."

"I'm Special Agent Drake, and this is my partner, Special Agent Luckman," Tom introduced them.

Her face softened. "You're the FBI agents."

"Yes, we are, ma'am. May we come in?" Tom asked.

"Of course." Avery's mother opened the door wider, then ushered them into a lounge room off the entrance foyer. "You can leave now, Leon," she growled at a young man in his twenties who was standing with his hands on his hips in the middle of the room.

"I'm not going anywhere." He glowered back.

"You're not welcome here!" Mrs. Ormont yelled.

"This isn't about you. This is about Avery," Leon retorted.

"If you cared about my daughter then you would have broken up with her when you could see that you were causing a rift between her and her family."

"If *you* cared about your daughter, you wouldn't keep trying to run her life. She's nineteen. She knows what she wants. We're happy together. You should be happy for her. You should be supporting her, not trying to ruin things for her."

She'd had enough of this childish arguing. "Enough," Chloe said firmly. "This isn't about either of you. This is about Avery, and standing here bickering like five-year-olds isn't going to help us get her back. Now, everyone sit."

Reluctantly, both Leon and Mrs. Ormont took seats, at opposite sides of the lounge room. Avery's mother went to sit next to her husband, who had been sitting quietly on one of the sofas, his head in his hands. While the others were channeling anger to keep their fear at bay, Mr. Ormont just looked lost.

Destroyed. Chloe couldn't imagine what it felt like to lose your only child this way.

"Now, who reported Avery missing?" she asked, surveying the group.

"I did," Leon replied. "She was supposed to call me last night, but she didn't. I thought she might have just fallen asleep early—between school and her job, she was exhausted. I thought I'd stop by early and surprise her, take her out to breakfast and then drop her off at work. When I got there, I saw all the smashed windows, and I knew something was wrong, so I called 911."

"You didn't call us," Mrs. Ormont muttered.

"*You* didn't even notice someone coming here and taking her," Leon shot back.

Before a bickering match could ensue again, Tom intervened. "Did you see or hear anything last night?" he asked Avery's parents.

Both shook their heads.

"We were out late at a dinner party at a friend's house. When we got back, we went straight up to bed," Mrs. Ormont said. "The next thing we knew, sirens and cop cars were coming down our driveway."

"Did you see anything when you got here?" Chloe asked Leon. She already knew he wouldn't have. The killer would have been waiting for Avery to get home and had grabbed her in the bath, but still, she had to ask.

"No," Leon said quietly. "I parked on the street because I knew her parents didn't approve of us dating. I came in around the back, and I didn't notice anything off until I got closer and saw the broken glass."

"What about over the last few days or weeks?" Tom asked. "Have you noticed anything strange? Anyone hanging around the house or at Avery's work or school? Has she mentioned anything? Emails or phone calls or messages that upset or worried her? Anyone following her?"

"I didn't see anything unusual," Mrs. Ormont said quietly. Her husband said nothing.

But Leon's brow crinkled.

"She did say something," he said slowly. "About a week ago. She had a late class, and she thought someone was following her to her car. It was just that one time and she never actually saw someone, but it freaked her out. She asked me to come and pick her up the next time she had a late class."

"She didn't see anyone?" Chloe pushed.

"No, she just thought she heard footsteps following her."

"She didn't see a car?" Tom asked.

"Just the footsteps following her," Leon repeated.

There was a chance that whoever had been following Avery that night had nothing to do with this case. She was a pretty, young woman. There could be any number of people who might have wanted to follow her for a variety of reasons. But that both Taylor and Avery had reported being followed shortly before their abductions had to mean something.

"She didn't tell me," Mrs. Ormond said quietly. Tears welled in her eyes and then began to trickle out. "Avery never told me that someone had followed her. She didn't tell me that she was scared. She didn't come to me. Why didn't she come to me?" Her face crumpled, and she began to sob as her façade broke away.

Chloe half expected Leon to jump in with some retort along the lines of her mother's interference in her life made Avery reluctant to come to her with problems. She expected her husband to snap out of his daze and comfort her.

Instead, it was the young man who stood and went to sit beside his girlfriend's mother. He put an arm around her shoulder. "Avery loves you so much," he told her. "Sometimes your meddling drives her crazy, but she adores you. She wanted the two of you to be friends, to continue to get closer as she gets older."

Mrs. Ormont gave him a grateful smile and leaned into him as she continued to weep.

Tragedy either brought people together or tore them apart.

For Leon and the Ormonts, it looked like it was making them closer.

For her and Fin, it had torn them apart.

She hoped there was a way to undo the damage that had been done.

* * * * *

10:52 A.M.

Fin wasn't looking forward to this.

At all.

He knew Chloe must be dreading it as much as he was. He knew she didn't want to keep seeing him, and he certainly didn't want to have to keep seeing her.

Being around her made him want to let go of his anger, but that was a mistake.

Anger was all that was holding back the pain.

He really shouldn't be so hurt that Chloe walked out. It wasn't like she was the first person in his life to do so. His mother had walked out on him when he was six. Fin still remembered the day vividly. She'd sat him and his little sister Samara down on the sofa and told them she was leaving. She'd offered no explanation, although when he'd gotten older, he had learned she hadn't left because she'd had an affair or fallen in love with someone else; she'd simply left because she wanted to. He had begged her to stay, wrapped his arms around her waist and cried and pleaded, but it hadn't done any good. She had simply walked out the door without a second glance.

If she had been the only person who left him, then that would be one thing.

But she wasn't.

His mother was just the first of many people to turn their back on him.

His father was next. He met a woman when Fin was eleven. At first, he had hated the idea of his dad dating, but then he'd rethought his stance and decided it would be nice to have a mom again.

Only that wasn't what his father's girlfriend had had in mind.

She didn't want stepkids.

She had four of her own, and after her husband had left, she was after someone to help her raise them. Shortly after his dad had proposed to her, she had convinced him that they couldn't care for six children and that no one could take hers, but maybe his parents could take his kids.

So, he and Samara had been sent to live with their grandparents.

Now thirteen and ten, both he and Samara had gone through a rebellious phase. They'd driven their grandparents to the edge, and after almost two years, his grandfather had had enough and bailed.

It wasn't until he'd almost lost his sister that he finally realized he was throwing his life away over people who couldn't have cared less. He'd stopped with the wild partying, he'd focused on his studies, was Valedictorian, and went on to study medicine.

Three people had turned their backs on him and walked away. Very nearly four if Samara had had her way.

If he were into that whole psychiatry thing, he'd probably admit he had some abandonment issues.

Maybe it was true.

He really didn't care.

All he knew was that Chloe had been just another person he'd loved who left, and he so badly wanted to hate her for it.

It would make things *so* much easier if he could hate her.

Right now, the best he could muster was anger.

And there was no way he was letting that go any time soon.

"Fin?"

"Yeah?" He blinked and looked at Taylor who was standing beside him, anxiously fiddling with the sleeves of her coat.

"What if I can't remember anything that will help them?"

He wrapped a reassuring arm around her shoulders. He may have had a lot of people walk out on him, but he wasn't turning his back on Taylor. He was here for her until her family arrived. Then he would do the right thing and step back. While he knew it would temporarily hurt her, long-term it was what was best for her. "You remember what you remember," he told her. "There's no pressure."

"Of course, there's pressure," she scoffed. "How are they going to find him if I can't give them something to point them in the right direction?"

"It's not your job to find him," he reminded her. "You're the victim, they're the FBI agents. It's their job to find him and arrest him."

Taylor said nothing, and he thought she was going to disagree with him again. She was upset that she didn't know enough about the man she had spent nineteen months with to send Tom and Chloe right to his door.

Fin suspected that obsessing over how helpful she was or wasn't being was helping keep her emotions about what had happened to her at bay. That wasn't a strategy that she could employ indefinitely. Sooner or later those emotions were going to come barreling out.

"Are you and Special Agent Luckman a couple?" Taylor asked in a rush, her gaze fixed firmly on his chest.

"No," he answered honestly. "Why do you ask?"

She shrugged. "I don't know. She looks at you funny. And the way you look at her. I thought that maybe you were together and just didn't want me to know."

He sighed. He didn't want to have this conversation with her. One, because she was suffering and he knew she was more attached to him than was healthy. Two, because it wasn't any of her business. And three, because he didn't like thinking about his relationship with Chloe, let alone talking about it. "We used to be, but we broke up," he told her.

"Oh," she said in a small voice like she didn't believe him.

"Look at me, Taylor." He waited until she reluctantly lifted her eyes to meet his. "Chloe and I broke up months ago, but she is a great agent, and there is no one I would trust more to solve your case."

That was true.

Whatever his and Chloe's problems, he knew how smart and detail-oriented she was. She was caring and kind and compassionate. And she loved her job. She would do anything and everything she could to solve a case. That made her a great agent, but it also meant that she was sometimes reckless. She wanted to catch the bad guys. He got that. And respected it. But sometimes she did things when she hadn't thought through all the consequences. She was so busy focusing on the end game that she forgot to make sure she got there safely. Although they weren't together anymore, he hoped that recklessness didn't end up hurting her.

A car pulled up in front of them, and Fin quickly guided Taylor to it.

It was time.

May as well get it over with as quickly as possible.

"How are you doing today, Taylor?" Tom asked as they got into the car.

"Fine, thank you," Taylor mumbled.

Chloe frowned at Taylor. "Is she wearing my clothes?"

"Her parents are bringing her some clothes when they arrive tonight, but she needed something to wear for today. She couldn't go in a hospital gown," he said defensively.

Part of him had known that bringing some of the clothes Chloe had left behind at their place when she'd moved out was a bad idea. He'd debated it briefly but decided that it couldn't be all that big of a deal since she'd left them behind anyway. And Taylor really *did* need something to wear.

There was also the chance he'd *wanted* to upset her.

It was cruel, he knew it.

But he was hurting, and he wanted to lash out, no matter how childish it was.

Chloe said nothing, simply gave him an inscrutable stare and then turned back around in her seat to stare out the front window.

They lapsed into uncomfortable silence during the short drive to his house. They were going to see if Taylor could retrace the path she'd taken when she'd escaped. If she could lead them back to the house where she'd been held, then they could find the man who'd abducted her. The man who had already taken a new victim.

Fin really hoped this worked, but he knew Taylor was afraid she wouldn't be able to remember which roads she'd run down. There was a genuine chance that she wouldn't be able to. She'd been running for her life. She had been running on a partially healed broken leg and been in pain. She hadn't been dressed for the cold night. She'd been in shock. Taking note of where she had been and where she was going had not been high on her priority list. All she'd wanted was to find safety.

She had found safety, but if they couldn't find her abductor, then she might not remain safe.

Still, what he'd told her earlier was true. There was no one else he would trust to find this vicious serial killer than Chloe.

"All right, Taylor, this is where you found Fin," Tom announced when he pulled the car to a stop. "Which direction were you coming from?"

Taylor looked up and down the street helplessly.

From the way she'd been staggering about, Fin knew this was never going to work. She hadn't seen any of her surroundings. Maybe if he helped her get started, something might come back to her. She had been out of it by the time she'd gotten to his street, but maybe she had been more cognizant earlier.

"She came up the street that way," he pointed.

Taylor shot him a grateful smile, and Tom drove down to the end of his block. "Which way now?" Tom asked.

Carefully considering, Taylor slowly pointed to the right. "I think I came this way."

Tom turned the car in that direction and continued slowly along the street. "Just tell me when I should turn and which way."

They trundled along for several blocks before Taylor called out, "Stop." Tom did, and Taylor pointed to the left. "I think I came up that way."

With her confidence growing, Taylor leaned forward in her seat, anxiously watching out the front window and sporadically instructing Tom to turn left or right. With each direction she gave, Fin's hope began to grow. Maybe Taylor really could do this. Maybe she really could lead them right to the place where she had been hurt and held prisoner.

"Where next?" Chloe asked after Taylor had remained quiet for a couple of blocks.

"I don't know," Taylor said, her head was whipping from side to side. "That way, I think." She pointed to the left. Then she shook her head. "No. It was that way," she changed her mind. "No. Left. It was definitely left."

Tom turned the car to the left, but they hadn't gone more than half a block when Taylor stopped them.

"Maybe it was right after all," she said. "I don't know. I don't remember."

Her anxiety levels were growing, and she flung open her door and jumped out of the car.

"I don't know," she cried helplessly. "I don't know where I came from. I was just running as fast as I could. All I wanted was to get away from him. I'm sorry. I wasn't paying attention. I should have been, but I wasn't."

"It's alright, Taylor," Fin assured her, having followed her from the car.

"Don't worry about it; it was worth a try," Tom consoled her.

"No. I should be able to help you. I *have* to help you. I have to. I'm sorry. I haven't given you anything yet. How will you stop him? He'll take someone else. He'll tie them to that table and use his machines and tools to break their bones, and there'll be nothing you can do to stop him." Taylor was crying in earnest now. "I can figure it out. I can. I'm sure I can. It was this way. Yes, this way." She began to run through the snow as fast as she could with a moon boot on her healing leg.

Fin ran after her, wrapping his arms around her and yanking her up against his chest. He held her tighter when she struggled. "It's okay, Taylor. It's okay," he soothed. This was a bad idea. She was putting too much pressure on herself. This wasn't helping her to heal.

"I'm sorry. I'm sorry," she sobbed over and over again as she wiggled around so she could wrap her arms around his waist and bury her face in his chest as she wept.

Just as she had the last time she had watched him comfort the crying woman in his arms, Chloe watched him with an odd expression on her face.

* * * * *

12:29 P.M.

"You've been uncharacteristically quiet."

Chloe ignored her partner, mainly because he was right.

She had been uncharacteristically quiet since they'd dropped Fin and Taylor Sallow back off at the hospital.

It wasn't that she was usually a chatterbox. Well, not a *huge* one, anyway, but she usually liked to talk through what was going on in the cases they were working. It wasn't often that she sat in the car in silence or kept her mouth shut as they walked back to their office or didn't say a word as they sat at their desks.

But today she was lost in thought.

Overanalyzing her every interaction with Fin to try to make sense out of it.

"I don't think Fin meant to hurt your feelings by giving some of your clothes to Taylor to wear," her partner said cautiously.

He was wrong.

She was pretty sure that Fin had intended to hurt her by doing that.

What other reason could he have for scrounging out the few clothes she'd left behind when she'd moved out and dressing Taylor in them and then parading the young woman around in front of her?

There weren't many things she hadn't brought with her. Just a few old clothes she no longer wore and hadn't had room for in her suitcases. Chloe couldn't imagine that Fin had kept them in the closet where she'd left them. She was surprised he hadn't thrown them away.

Did it mean something that he'd kept them?

Had he been unable to part with them and held on to them as a reminder of her, a final thing to hold on to since she was gone?

Although she might wish that were true, that it might give her hope that a part of Fin still cared for her, Chloe believed he had most likely forgotten about the clothes. And then when this opportunity had presented itself, he'd decided it was a good way to lash out at her.

Or maybe she was just being completely egotistical and conceited to think he was even thinking of her at all.

Too many nights without good sleep were making her brain useless mush.

Tom had been a lot more tactful about finding out the details of what had gone down between her and her ex than she had been about finding out the details of his past with Hannah. She'd come right out and asked him how he knew Hannah just hours after the robbery at her store that had reunited the two of them. Tom hadn't been particularly forthcoming with answers, although he had eventually relayed the details of the night that had ripped him and Hannah apart.

Thankfully he hadn't done that to her.

Of course, he knew that they'd broken up. And he knew it was because of their baby's death. But he didn't know the details of why exactly she had left.

Chloe wasn't even sure *she* knew why she had left.

Although she appreciated him keeping his questions to himself up until now, she hoped he wasn't going to start to pry.

She didn't want to talk about her and Fin.

There *was* no her and Fin to talk about.

All there was, was the jealousy she felt every time she saw him holding Taylor in his arms as the young woman cried, and the knowledge that if he would take her, she wanted him back.

"Really," Tom continued when she didn't say anything. "Fin is a good guy, and I don't think he'd hurt you on purpose."

Normally, she would have agreed.

But Fin was so angry with her.

It was written all over his face every time they were in the same room together.

Chloe didn't know how to make his anger go away, or if she even had the right to ask him to let it go and give her a second chance.

She knew she'd hurt him badly. She knew she was just another person in his life who had walked away from him. She was sorry she had, but she hadn't felt like she had a choice. It had been the only way she could survive. If she'd stayed, she would have destroyed herself.

"Chloe—"

"Stop," she interrupted. "I'm fine. I'm not thinking about Fin right now." Okay, that was a lie, and she knew her partner knew it from the look on his face, but she just didn't want to talk about Fin with Tom. He didn't get it. He and Hannah had never stopped loving each other. They hadn't hurt each other; they'd just been hurting and unable to deal with things. It was different with her and Fin.

"Okay." Tom nodded. "Back to the case, then."

Yes.

The case would help to clear her head.

Work was the one constant in her life that she could count on. It wasn't going anywhere, and that gave her a sense of stability.

"I was thinking about something Taylor said today," she announced.

"What, specifically?" Tom asked.

"She said, 'He'll tie them to that table and use his machines and tools to break their bones, and there'll be nothing you can do to stop him,'" she quoted verbatim. She didn't quite have a photographic memory, but she was pretty close, and usually remembered things in great detail—particularly quotes. *Especially* quotes from witnesses or suspects.

"That got you thinking of something?"

"Well, she said he tied her up, and earlier she was telling us about the room where she was kept. She mentioned a 'weird-looking bench type thing with a whole bunch of leather straps attached to it.' I was thinking that might be some sort of modified examining table. Like from a hospital or doctor's office."

"You're thinking the killer could be a doctor," Tom stated.

"I do," she confirmed, seeing in her partner's brown eyes that he had come to the same conclusion.

"It makes sense given that he likes to break bones but appears to take measures to set them, so they heal before he moves on to breaking another bone."

"And what Taylor said about him using machines and tools, what if he has an x-ray machine? Some of the bones that had been broken on Kelly Mitchell and Christie Neil were small, individual bones in their feet and hands, and specific ribs. What if he uses the x-ray to help make sure he gets the exact bone he wants, and then he uses it after to make sure its set. He needs to set the bones because he doesn't want anything to kill them before he's ready. At least, that's his goal."

"That does make sense. We could look into any individual who's purchased one."

"Medical tools, too," she added. "I was thinking that since some of the bones he's broken in his victims are small, he'd need to be careful breaking them. In the autopsies, every single broken bone was at a different stage of healing. He did them one at a time, so to do a little bone in their hand or foot would be tricky. What if he used one of those things surgeons use when they do a rhinoplasty—"

"An osteotome," Tom inserted.

"Why do you know the name of that?" she asked.

Tom shrugged. "I know a lot of useless trivia."

"Okay." She huffed a small laugh. "Well, if he used something like that and a hammer, that would help him break individual small bones."

"The bones broken in each of our three victims are different," Tom said. "He doesn't start at one point and then work his way around the body. How does he choose them?"

There was no way to get an answer to that question until they caught the killer. And even then, he might not offer them any answers. Or they wouldn't get a chance to even ask him questions; if he didn't want to spend the rest of his life in prison, he could always play the suicide or suicide-by-cop card.

"If we are looking for a doctor, possibly even a surgeon, we should start at the hospital. We could talk to Fin," she suggested cautiously. "See if there's anyone he thinks we should look into."

Her partner raised a knowing eyebrow.

He obviously thought she was looking for an excuse to spend time around her ex.

Maybe she was.

But it also made sense.

If this guy really was a doctor, they were going to have to start looking for him somewhere. The hospital was as good a place as any to start with their search. And if they were going to the hospital anyway, then why not start with a doctor they knew?

And if in doing that, she got to spend a bit of extra time around Fin, then that was just an added bonus. Maybe if they spent some time together, where there was no pressure to discuss their shared history, then she might be able to make some headway in getting Fin to forgive her.

Right about now Chloe was up for taking advantage of any opportunity—no matter how small—to try and mend fences with the man she still loved.

* * * * *

3:15 P.M.

She was wearing the reindeer beanie.

That was the first thing Fin thought when he saw Chloe climb out of the car.

Despite the anger he still felt toward her, his lips curved up at the corners into a small smile. She always looked so adorably sexy when she wore that silly beanie.

His eyes roamed down her body, and he wondered what other Christmassy articles of clothing she was wearing under her sensible black suit and white shirt. Did she have on her candy cane socks? Or those panties with the reindeer, or the bra with Santa Claus on one cup and Mrs. Claus on the other? She liked to dress professionally when she was at work, but she could never resist having some item of Christmas clothing on.

Fin remembered the first time he'd seen her in all her crazy Christmas clothes. It was the first Christmas they'd spent together, and they'd been dating only a month or so. It had been a couple of days after Halloween—in his mind way too early to start thinking about Christmas. But it wasn't for Chloe. She'd been wearing red and white candy cane striped stockings, a bright red dress with a Santa village motif, a red cloak with fluffy white around the hood, and red mittens with white snowflakes. She'd looked ridiculous and sexy and impossibly sweet all mixed together.

He chuckled at the memory. She could be so goofy sometimes, and she just couldn't help herself when it came to Christmas things, especially Christmas clothes. As soon as she'd told him she was pregnant, she'd started buying Christmas outfits for the baby.

Abruptly, he sobered.

Their baby was gone, and so was Chloe.

Their relationship was over.

Reminiscing about the past was only going to cause him more pain.

Fin straightened and moved away from the emergency room door. Whatever Chloe and Tom were doing here, he didn't care. Taylor's parents had arrived an hour ago; she was no longer his concern, and neither was this case.

He had turned and headed back to the desk to collect another patient chart—his shift was over, but he wasn't ready to go home yet—when he heard Tom call his name. He really wanted to ignore them. To keep going, go back to work, make it through the holidays, then move on with his life.

He did *not* want Chloe and Tom to drag him into their case.

It was nothing to do with him.

Okay, so he'd stumbled upon Taylor as she staggered toward his house, but that was it. He didn't know anything. Talking to him was just wasting their time.

"Taylor is with her parents," he told them when they approached.

"We know," Tom said. "We wanted to talk to *you*."

"I don't have anything to tell you." Why couldn't they just leave him alone? It was torture being around Chloe again. Especially around this time of year when memories of happier times kept barging their way into his mind.

"Can we go someplace more private?" Tom asked.

Fin sighed. May as well get this over with. "We can go in here." He led them to a small office next to the staff lounge and sank tiredly down into a chair.

He had taken the chair closest to the door, and as Chloe walked past him, he caught a whiff of her perfume.

They said smell was the sense with the strongest connection to memory, and true to this, memories of Chloe began to flash through his mind.

The way she nibbled on her toast every morning with impossibly small bites so that it took her ten minutes to eat a slice. The way she was always cold and liked to sit on his lap in winter when they hung out on the couch and binge watched their favorite shows before bed. The way she giggled in her sleep, her face lighting up in the most breathtaking smile. The way her bottom lip wobbled when she was trying not to cry. The way her eyes crinkled at the sides when she frowned at him, making her look so sweet, it was hard to continue the argument. The way she laughed every time he tried to give her a massage to get her in the mood because her stomach and back were so ticklish.

There were *so* many things he loved about her that when he thought of them all, it was hard to remember why he was angry with her.

"Fin."

He'd been so lost in thought, he hadn't bothered to listen to whatever they were saying. He had to get it together. So, he still loved Chloe; he knew that already.

Sometimes love wasn't enough.

And he was tired of rehashing his feelings for her in his mind. He was tired of justifying to himself why he was angry with her.

He was tired of hurting and grieving not just the loss of their child, but of the loss of their relationship, as well.

It was time to answer their questions, send them on their way, and be done with it.

"Yeah?"

"How's Taylor?" Tom asked.

Fin saw Chloe's flinch because he was looking for it.

There was no doubt about it, she was jealous of his relationship with Taylor. Which was ridiculous because he didn't *have* a relationship with Taylor.

Why would she be jealous?

She had been the one to end their relationship and walk out on him, not the other way around.

But it was pretty clear that she was, and if she was jealous, it had to be because she still had feelings for him. If she didn't, she wouldn't care who he was with.

Maybe she still loved him.

Then why leave?

Whatever.

She *had* left.

And even if she did still love him, that didn't change anything.

"She's doing okay; her parents finally arrived," he replied.

"How did she do when you left?" Tom asked. "Is she coping okay with the idea that her parents are there to support her now, not you? She was getting pretty attached."

Taylor had *not* been happy when he'd said goodbye.

She'd cried and screamed and begged, and walking out the door had been one of the hardest things he had ever done. But it was what she needed. He couldn't be there for her forever, and the quicker they made the transition from her depending on him to her depending on her family, the better.

"She didn't do well. In the end, Eric went in to give her a tranquilizer. We decided it was best that I don't go and see her again. The more I hang around, the harder it is for her to make the switch."

Although he knew that in his head, his heart still felt horrible for walking away when she needed him. He knew what it was like to have the people who you relied on disappear and the internal scramble to try to find a new safe place and sense of balance. He hated to put Taylor through that on the back of the trauma she had suffered, but what choice did he have?

"If you want to talk to Taylor again, you need to check with Eric. I didn't ask what he gave her, so I'm not sure whether she'll be awake, or capable of being interviewed," he told them.

"We need to talk to *you*," Chloe said quietly.

"Me? Why?" Fin couldn't think of anything useful he could tell them about the serial killer who abducted women and broke their bones. Maybe they weren't here about that. Maybe it was another case. "Is this about Taylor's case or another one?"

"Taylor's," Chloe replied.

"What do you want to ask me?"

"The precision with which he breaks his victims' bones, and what Taylor said about him using machines and tools, makes us think we're looking for a doctor," she told him.

A doctor?

It made sense.

He had seen Taylor's x-rays, and if he had to guess, it looked like someone with some medical knowledge had hurt her. A doctor, radiologist, nurse, physical therapist, possibly even someone with veterinarian knowledge, could have done it.

"You think it's someone here at the hospital?" he asked. How creepy would it be if he had been working alongside a serial killer?

"Possibly," Tom answered. "We thought we'd start here, see if there was anyone you can think of who might be capable of this."

Fin considered that.

No one immediately sprang to mind.

"Anyone who might have taken a particular interest in Taylor and her case. Anyone who talked about the cases a lot. Anyone who you just get a bad vibe from?" Chloe prompted.

There was no one who had asked questions about Taylor other than those who were involved in treating her, and no one he could think of who had talked a lot about the case, but there *was* someone from whom he got a bad vibe from. Well, two people, actually.

"You thought of someone?" Tom asked, seemingly sensing his train of thought.

"Two people. One I know personally, the other I've only heard about."

"Who are they?" Chloe asked, eager anticipation in her brown eyes.

"There's a doctor here at the hospital named Harley Zabkar. He's an orthopedic surgeon who would certainly fit with your profile. There's just something about him I don't like. I never have. He's terrible to patients and their families; there are several complaints on file about him. And he's hard to work with—he's rude and arrogant. But he is good at what he does, which I suppose is why he still has a job. I know that doesn't sound like a lot, but it's the look he has on his face when he consults down here in the ER. When he talks about a patient, there's no compassion, no empathy on his face. He's not just neutral either. It's like he's excited that they were hurt. I don't know how to explain it."

"And the other man?" Tom asked.

"One of the nurses who recently transferred here was in a bad car accident a few years ago. She went through extensive physical therapy at a private facility about twenty minutes from here. She said one of the therapists there was overly interested in her and her injuries. Whenever he was there, he would grill her about which bones she had broken, and what it felt like, and how they had healed. She said it wasn't just her, but he was always asking inappropriate questions about patients' injuries, specifically broken bones. I think his name is Pete Larkin."

* * * * *

4:02 P.M.

"Thanks for your help, Fin," Chloe said. It felt weird to say his name again; it had been so long since the two of them had spent any time together. She liked this, and she didn't want it to end. She wanted to think up more questions to ask just so that she and Tom didn't have to leave yet, but her partner had already covered everything they needed to know for their case.

"Anything I can do to help catch this guy," he said, although he addressed his statement more to Tom than to her.

Fin had barely glanced her way the whole time they'd been talking to him. Even when she asked him a question, he kept his gaze focused on her partner.

But ...

Chloe thought that he might have breathed in her perfume when they'd first walked into the office.

She *thought* he might have, but she wasn't completely sure.

One thing she *was* completely sure of was that Fin was still angry with her.

Very angry.

So angry she was starting to think that there was no hope for them. That her walking away and breaking his heart was irreparable. She should have known better. She should have talked to him, explained things.

But she hadn't, and now Fin hated her.

Still, he had been affected by the scent of her perfume. Chloe had been able to tell by the glazed look in his eyes that he was reminiscing. He hadn't looked angry as he'd been lost in thought, so hopefully, he had been thinking about happy times. And if he was thinking about happy times, then maybe there *was* still a chance for them.

Even if there was only the slimmest of chances that she and Fin could repair their relationship, she had to try.

After all, it was Christmastime.

A time for miracles and love and hope and second chances.

That had to mean something.

"Let us know if you think of anything else," Tom was saying to Fin as they both stood.

She stood too—somewhat uncertainly. She wanted to talk to Fin, but she was afraid he was going to turn her down flat. Maybe it was best just to move on. It had to be the healthier option for both of them.

Chloe followed her partner out the door, but then she froze.

Now was not the time to be a coward. If she wanted to get back what she and Fin had lost, then she had to fight for them.

"Wait."

Tom turned and looked at her, confused. "Did you forget something?"

"No. I uh, I just need a minute," she said, looking back at the door.

"Ah." Tom nodded understandingly. "Sure. I'll go see if the nurse Fin told us about is working tonight, then I'll call and check in on Hannah. She wasn't feeling well this morning. Meet you in the car."

She watched her partner walk away. Chloe remembered when Fin used to fuss over her when she was sick. He'd make sure she stayed tucked up in bed. He'd cook her favorite pumpkin soup for her; he'd read to her, and he'd hover and fuss and take care of her until she was better. She missed that.

Taking a deep breath, she prepared herself; she shouldn't be this nervous to talk to the man she still loved, but she was. She turned the door handle, but before she could push it open, it opened itself.

Fin was right there on the other side.

Since she hadn't been expecting that, her balance was thrown off, and she stumbled slightly, brushing against Fin as she did.

Goose bumps broke out all over her skin, and it felt as if her heart stopped beating for a moment.

This was where she was supposed to be—with Fin. She'd been stupid to run from happiness in the wake of the death of their baby. She should have clung to the one person who was grieving as much as she was.

Why had she thrown it all away?

Fin was everything she had dreamed about in a partner. Kind, caring, compassionate, strong. He made her feel like a princess like she was the most important person on the planet. The way he heated her clothes in front of the fireplace for her in the mornings during the wintertime because he knew she always got cold. How when it was raining and he dropped her off at work, he would always get out and hold an umbrella over her head as he walked her to the door. That he always left her little notes on the fridge, especially if they missed each other between his crazy hours at the hospital and her crazy hours at the FBI.

She loved him so much. Why had she let him go?

"Chloe." He was clicking his fingers in front of her face. "Are you okay?" Concern crinkled his brow as he watched her carefully.

She had to fight not to let tears spill out as they filled her eyes. "Fine," she assured him.

He didn't look convinced. "Did you forget something?" His gaze moved to the table where they'd been sitting which was empty save for the dirty coffee cups that had been there when they got here.

"No." She fiddled nervously with the Christmas charm bracelet she wore all throughout December. She'd never been anxious around Fin before, but now that she knew that everything she said or did could either help bring them together or push them farther apart, she was obsessing over every little thing. "I miss you," she said in a rush, going with straight honesty before she could overthink things and wind up being a coward and saying nothing at all.

At her words, Fin froze.

Like he had been turned into a statue.

Her nervousness growing, Chloe began to babble. "I never meant to hurt you. I mean, I know that I did. And given your history, I shouldn't have left the way I did. Only I wasn't thinking properly then. I just knew, well, that I needed time to think. But it's been months, and I miss you. I didn't realize how much until I saw you again, but now that I have, I know I made a mistake. A *big* mistake. And I know I don't have any right to ask you to forgive me, but I *am* sorry. So sorry. I would never hurt you on purpose. You know that. I was thinking that maybe we could go out to dinner?" she finished.

Fin said nothing.

Chloe held her breath, waiting, her heart hammering in her chest.

Why wasn't he saying anything?

His blue eyes were cold, unforgiving.

"Is this because you're jealous of Taylor?" His tone was harsh, nothing like the Fin she knew.

His words stung. Not so much because of his hard voice and even harder expression, but because it was clear he *wanted* to hurt her.

She had known that she'd hurt him when she'd walked away. She deserved to stand here and take his anger. He was lashing out at her, and she couldn't really fault him for it.

Straightening her spine, she looked him directly in the eye. "No. It's because I miss you." She took a deep breath and admitted, "It's because I still love you."

Chloe had expected him to say or do something at her admission, preferably pull her into his arms, sweep her off her feet, kiss her and tell her he still loved her, too.

But he did none of those things.

He just stood there, glowering at her as the dark, angry, man he'd become.

"It's over, Chloe. Our baby died, you left, we've both moved on. I don't want to see you again."

His words were like a slap in the face.

If she was honest, she hadn't really expected the sweeping her off her feet and proclamation of love, but she hadn't expected this, either. She had thought he might meet her halfway, or even come a quarter of the way. But she'd expected him to give her something. Just one little thing to convince her that he still cared.

"B-but—" she stuttered.

"No." He cut her off harshly. "No buts. Goodbye, Chloe."

With that, he turned and walked away without a second glance.

She stood there in shock.

Had that really just happened?

Had she really just taken a leap of faith and laid her heart on the line for him to just stomp all over it and walk away?

She was crushed.

She hadn't hurt this bad since the day her son had died.

It was really over.

Even though she hadn't realized it until this moment, part of her had always believed that after a little time, after they'd grieved the loss of their baby, that they would find their way back to one another.

How naïve could she be?

And how stupid.

She had no one to blame but herself.

It had been her choice to walk away, and now she had to pay the price.

Sinking down into one of the chairs, she propped her elbows up on the table, buried her face in her hands and cried.

* * * * *

6:47 P.M.

Why her?

What about her had made him pick her out of all the other young women in the city?

If Avery knew why he'd chosen her, then maybe she could figure out a way to talk her way out of this room.

She had tried being obedient.

She had tried to make a run for it.

But in the end, there was nothing she could do to stop him from hurting her.

He hadn't held back in telling her exactly what he intended to do to her. Strap her down to the examining table in the corner, then break every bone in her body one at a time until he'd broken them all and killed her, or until her body couldn't take anymore and she died.

Avery knew she had to get out of here, but how?

He had let her search every inch of wall and floor in her frantic investigation of the room. If he was happy to let her do that, it was because he knew she wasn't going to find a way out. After he'd left her alone here, she had examined the room at a much slower, more methodical pace and come to the same conclusion.

She was trapped.

That didn't leave her with many options.

It seemed highly unlikely she was going to be able to convince him to let her go. He'd done this three times before, and those women hadn't been able to talk their way to freedom, so why should she be any different?

Although she didn't want to admit it, it seemed her only hope was probably to pray that the cops were able to find her before he killed her.

But again, that hadn't worked for the three women who had been here before her.

Avery was sure they had prayed for a savior.

A savior that never came.

Still, she couldn't give up. She couldn't just lie back and let him slowly kill her, broken bone by broken bone. It wasn't in her nature to just lie back and take things.

He may have kidnapped her; he may have locked her away here; he may be going to hurt her; he may have all the power, but there was one little thing she still had control over.

How she chose to act.

She could be the compliant little doll he wanted her to be, or she could fight him every step of the way.

Fighting presented serious challenges. He had warned her of the consequences of disobeying him. He wouldn't set the breaks, and he wouldn't give her anything for the pain if she fought him.

Obeying would be the safer option.

She just wasn't sure she could do it.

How could she just *let* him hurt her and do nothing to stop it from happening?

Even if it was pointless, she had to try.

Avery just had to ready herself for the pain. She didn't have a very high threshold for physical pain; she usually had to dope herself up on painkillers after getting a shot, but now she had to be strong.

She heard the sound of the door opening, and her resolve instantly wavered.

Could she really do this?

What choice did she have?

She could roll over and do nothing, or she could do what she could to fight back. Maybe if she was lucky, the lack of treatment of her broken bones might even lead her to a quick—albeit painful—death.

That was something she had never imagined would cross her mind, but it was her new reality.

Pain and a slow death or pain and a quick death. There was pain either way, so she may as well at least hope that the end was hastened.

Avery expected to see the man carrying another plate of food. He'd brought her three meals already, and although she was his prisoner, he certainly didn't feed her like one. For breakfast, he'd brought her a tray full of French toast, waffles, pancakes, fruit, toast, and an array of cereals. Lunch had been a huge salad sandwich with French fries. And dinner had been lasagna with a side of steamed vegetables. It was clear it was important to him that she remain as physically healthy as possible. He wanted her alive. He wanted her to survive. He wanted to achieve his goal of breaking every bone in a living victim's body.

But this time, he didn't have food in his hands.

"Evening, Avery." He smiled at her. It was a weird smile. Not creepy per se, but not warm either—more arrogant and condescending. He liked having the upper hand; it made him feel strong. He was a big guy, and she was barely five foot one; it didn't prove that he was a strong guy to be able to hurt her.

Avery offered no response since she wasn't sure what the right one was. It seemed the better option was to just remain silent for now.

Besides, she needed to focus.

She may as well attempt to make a dash for freedom every time one presented itself.

He had put the key in a pocket inside his sweater. The chances of her getting to it were pretty slim, but she was going to try anyway.

"It's time to roll the dice," he announced.

She didn't know what that meant, but she knew it was nothing good. She'd thought she would have more time before he started his broken bone quest. Obviously, she was wrong. He was ready and raring to get going.

"Let's see how lucky you are today." He pulled a large dice from a pocket and tossed it from hand to hand. "Ones are for feet, twos are for legs, threes are for hands, fours are for arms, fives for the torso, and six for the face."

It took a moment for what he'd just said to sink in.

When it did, she could feel her blood pressure rising.

He meant that whatever number it landed on, he would break a bone from that part of her body.

With another smile, he tossed the dice in the air and let it drop to the floor where it bounced a couple of times before rolling to a stop under the table.

"Go get it, see what your number is," he instructed.

Avery complied.

She wanted him to think she was some docile little girl who was going to do whatever he said whenever he said to do it. That way he wouldn't see her coming.

She walked to the table, stooped, and looked at the dice.

"What number did you get?" he asked before she could pick it up, coming to stand behind her, presumably in case she lied. What was the point in lying? None of her options were any good.

"Three," she replied. What was that again? Hands? Depending on what he chose, that shouldn't be too debilitating. If he'd broken her leg, she wouldn't have been able to do much, but a hand still left her with options.

"You got lucky, a broken finger isn't such a bad place to start. Bring me the dice."

Avery scooped it up and started toward him, pretending she intended to do what he asked. At the last second, she launched herself at him, aiming her shoulder right for his stomach. If she could just stun him long enough to get the key, she could run. Run and not stop until she was far, far away from here.

She threw her entire weight at him, but instead of knocking him down, she simply bounced straight back off him.

For a moment, she was stunned.

She'd given it everything she had, and he hadn't even staggered.

A hand clamped painfully down on her shoulder, and she was

spirited across the room, where he lifted her easily onto the examining table. Although she struggled wildly, it didn't seem to faze him, and in less than a minute, he had her firmly secured.

Tears stung the backs of her eyes.

This was hopeless.

How could she fight him when he was so much bigger than her?

And in a couple of minutes, she would be injured. He hadn't told her how long he waited in between bone breaks. Would he let her fully recover or just give her a couple of days or a week or two and then move on to the next one?

The man picked up her right hand, which unbeknownst to him was lucky for her because she was left-handed. He felt along her thumb, settling on the top bone.

"This didn't have to hurt, you know. You could have had a local anesthetic, a morphine drip. But you chose not to be a good girl, and now you have to suffer the consequences."

Then he picked up a small hammer, positioned it carefully, then lifted it and swung it down in one fluid motion.

She was sure she heard the snap of the bone breaking.

The pain was swift and sudden.

Avery could feel her heartbeat getting louder and louder until it seemed to reverberate through the room, the sound deafening.

The world shimmered around her, then dissolved into nothingness.

* * * * *

7:36 P.M.

He felt like scum.

Maybe he shouldn't have been so hard on Chloe.

Okay. Fine. Fin knew he *definitely* shouldn't have been so hard on Chloe.

He knew he was being unfair to her and yet, he couldn't let go of his anger. He knew that Chloe had suffered the same loss he had, that they had both been grieving when she left, but it was the walking away that killed him.

When they had needed each other most, she turned her back on him.

Even if he could forgive her and let go of the anger, how could he trust her again?

Is this what she was going to do every time something bad happened—just leave? Fin knew he couldn't take that.

He'd had enough people walk away from him in his life that he could never take Chloe back knowing that at any moment, she could do the same thing. He would live in a constant paralyzing fear that after every argument she would walk out the door. Or every time she didn't get her way. Or what if they lost another baby? Or if they had children and one of them got sick or hurt. Or if one of them lost their job or they had financial troubles. There were so many things that could go wrong, and he couldn't live knowing that any one of them could send Chloe packing again.

There was no way he was subjecting himself to that. Or any potential children they may have had.

He and Chloe were done.

There was no chance of them reconciling.

He knew that. He was even okay with it, although it did hurt.

So why was he feeling so awful?

Fin sighed and swirled the coffee in his cup.

He knew why he felt so awful. It was because he'd been deliberately mean to Chloe. He had wanted to hurt her like she'd hurt him. Which was childish and pathetic, and he was pretty sure it made him a terrible person.

He knew he had to remember that Chloe had been grieving, too, and she hadn't deliberately left to hurt him.

Tonight, she had offered him an olive branch, and he'd thrown it back in her face. She'd said she loved him and he'd lashed out. Wasn't that what he wanted? For her to still love him?

Maybe it would be easier to forgive her if she hadn't pulled away from him so soon after their son died, but it had been almost instantaneous. It made him wonder if she had wanted out of the relationship before that but felt trapped because of the pregnancy. Then once their baby was gone, there was nothing tying her to him anymore, so she had run.

Neither of them had been ready for the news that Chloe was pregnant. They hadn't been planning on having kids with him just finishing up his residency and Chloe just starting her career in the FBI. They'd been shocked to know that they were going to have a baby.

Shocked but happy.

At least, that's what he had thought.

But maybe he'd been wrong all along.

Maybe Chloe hadn't been all that happy to have something that would tie her to him forever.

Fin knew he should cut her some slack. She'd been in a lot of physical pain from the accident as well as the emotional pain from the loss they had both just suffered, but the fact that she'd withdrawn so quickly filled him with so many doubts.

None of those doubts excused his harsh treatment of her tonight.

Perhaps it would have been good for both of them to lay the past to rest. To make peace, maybe even remain friends, so they could both get closure and be able to move on with their lives.

Instead, he'd made her cry.

He knew that because he'd heard her as he'd stood outside the office door, an internal struggle raging inside him. Should he go back inside and accept her apology and let her down gently, or should he leave things as they were where he'd made it clear to her that it was over between them?

In the end, he had taken the coward's route and fled.

Not that he'd fled very far.

He was holed up in the doctor's lounge, not wanting to go home to the house he had shared with Chloe—the house where the nursery for their son was still just as it had been the day of the accident. The house that was so full of memories that they seemed to burst right out every time he opened the door. Fin hated staying in the house, and yet he couldn't leave it.

Tossing back his head, he drank the now cold coffee in one long gulp.

May as well call it a night.

As he opened the door, Fin was surprised to see Chloe just walking out of the office where they'd been talking earlier.

What was she still doing here?

It was almost eight, nearly four hours since he'd left her in tears.

An overwhelming need to go to her filled him.

He hated to see her cry. It ate at him, taking a little piece of his heart with every tear that fell. He wanted to hold her in his arms, wipe away her tears, and promise her that everything would be okay. He wanted to wash away the last seven months with all their hurt and grief and anger and doubts like they never happened.

His feet began moving before his brain even registered what he was doing.

"Fin."

He stopped and turned to see Eric Abbott approaching him.

By the time he turned back around, Chloe had disappeared. Part of him wanted to chase after her, but maybe it was a sign. Okay, he'd given her a harsher final nail in the coffin of their relationship than he had intended—or should have—but at least now it was done. She wasn't going to be holding out hope for something that was never going to happen, and he felt like he had taken the first step toward letting go of his anger.

"What's up?" he asked, turning back to his friend and colleague.

"It's Taylor," Eric replied.

"What about her?"

"She's freaking out."

"What do you want me to do about that?" They had all agreed—he, Eric, Taylor's parents—that it was best if he made a clean break with her. Dragging things out or coming back when she manipulated to get her way wasn't productive.

"She had a nightmare."

"Did she remember something? If she did, then you really want Tom and Chloe."

"No, she didn't remember something, but she woke up in a panic. She's hysterical, but she won't let anyone near her. She threw her family out of the room, and every time I try to go in, she gets worse. I think you need to go and see if you can calm her down."

He shook his head. "That's counterproductive, and you know it. Am I going to come running every time she asks for me? I feel sorry for her, and I hope she can find a way to get through this, but I can't be there for her long term. You know that. Her family knows that. She needs to start leaning on them and not me. If I do this, I'm telling her that she can get me to come back whenever she chooses. How long are we supposed to let that go on for? I know it's hard for her, but I think I would be doing more harm than good if I go in there."

"You're her safe place right now, Fin; maybe she needs you while we transition her across to her parents. What if we work on you going in there, giving her that sense of peace and stability that she needs, and then we'll have her parents go in. That way she's not completely relying on you."

Although he still thought he was right and that this was not actually going to help Taylor's recovery, he knew he'd do it. How could he not? She'd been through something so horrific, and even though he was afraid he was only actually making things worse by continuing to be her safe place, he couldn't leave her alone.

"Okay."

"Thanks."

Fin cast one last look at the emergency room doors. Was it too late to go and find Chloe or was she already gone?

"You know she still loves you," Eric said quietly.

"I know."

"You still love her too."

"I do."

"Then do something about it." Eric sounded both perplexed and annoyed.

"I can't."

"Why? Because you're still angry with her? You know she left because she was grieving and didn't know how else to handle her feelings." Eric also knew the pain of losing a child, and the results for his family had almost been catastrophic. His wife had fallen hard and fast into depression and ended up attempting suicide.

"It's not that simple," Fin said quietly. His and Eric's situations weren't the same. Eric and Lila may have pulled apart initially, and Lila may have struggled to get through things on her own while pushing her husband away … Anger had raged on both sides as they had blamed each other—but in the end, neither of them had walked away, and over time—and with hard work—they had rebuilt their family.

But it wasn't just anger standing between him and Chloe.

There was another insurmountable obstacle.

Guilt.

* * * * *

8:18 P.M.

It is over.

It is over.

It is over.

Chloe kept repeating that to herself so that maybe she could start accepting it.

Fin's rejection stung.

Okay, it was more like a knife slicing through her chest and gouging into her heart, shredding it to pieces.

At least now she knew for sure. There was no chance that she and Fin were going to get back together. He was too angry with her. There was nothing she could do to take back what she'd done. She had hurt him badly when she'd left, and no amount of apologies were going to change that.

So, she had to find a way to be okay with it.

It was time to move on.

While she was hurt by Fin's cold and harsh attitude, at least he'd been clear. He didn't want her back. He didn't love her anymore. He had already moved on with his life, putting his relationship with her in the past.

Now she had to do the same.

Step one was getting some answers.

She needed to sort out her feelings about her son's death and why it had made her push away the man she loved.

Chloe knocked on the door, her breathing accelerating as she waited for it to open. Was she sure she wanted to do this?

"Hi, Chloe. I'm Charlie, come on in." A smiling middle-aged man introduced himself as he opened the door. Dr. Charlie Abbott was in his early forties. He was tall, had short brown hair, brown eyes that were warm and empathetic, and a body that clearly showed he worked out.

He didn't wait to see if she was going to enter his office. He just turned and headed back to his desk, pausing to open what looked like a small refrigerator.

She stood right where she was.

"Come in if you want, or you can leave; whatever suits."

Charlie said it like it made no difference to him either way, but she knew he was testing her. He knew—just as she did—that the only way therapy was going to work was if she wanted it to. And if she couldn't even make herself walk in the door, then how was this going to be successful?

She shook herself.

This *had* to be successful.

Things might be over with Fin, but she didn't want to give up on love. She wanted to get married one day, have more kids, grow old with the man who owned her heart by her side.

If she wanted to have those things, then she needed to do this.

Determinedly she stepped inside the office, closing the door behind her.

Charlie pulled something out of his fridge. "You want a drink?" he asked over his shoulder.

"Water please." She wasn't really thirsty, but the drink would be a helpful distraction.

"Sure thing." He set a bottle of water on his desk, then dropped into a chair and unscrewed a bottle of apple juice.

"Uh, thanks," she said, nervous now that she was actually here. The idea of seeing a shrink had seemed a lot easier before she'd arrived. Now that she was here, she had to talk—only she didn't know what to say.

The doctor said nothing, just watched her closely. She could practically see the wheels turning in his head as he tried to figure her out and get a read on her.

Quickly she hurried to one of the chairs on the other side of his desk and plopped down into it. She didn't want him trying to figure her out. The idea that someone else could know more about what went on inside her head than she did made her uncomfortable.

Chloe wasn't sure what happened next.

It was clear Charlie didn't intend to lead the conversation. He was going to let her start and presumably say as much or as little as she wanted.

She both appreciated his approach and was terrified by it.

If it was up to her to start things off, she had no idea what to say. She'd come here because she needed help figuring out how her son's death had affected her. If she knew the answer to that, she wouldn't be here.

"Ah, thank you for seeing me on such short notice," she said. It was a stall tactic, but she needed a couple more moments to gather herself.

"You're welcome."

Deciding she may as well just jump off the cliff and plunge right in, Chloe asked, "Have you ever lost someone really close to you?"

"My nephew," he replied immediately. "He was five when he was killed, and it was a horrendous time for my family. Watching my brother and sister-in-law fall apart was hell. I wanted to help them, but I couldn't. That was the most helpless I have ever felt in my life. One of my very good friends lost her husband while she was pregnant, and although I hadn't been close with her husband, watching her grieve is the second most helpless I've ever felt. But I haven't lost a child if that's what you mean. My wife Savannah and I have three children; triplets, actually. And although things were a little difficult when they were born, they were never really in danger of not surviving. So, no, I don't know how you feel; I've never gone through that."

Chloe absorbed that. She liked Charlie's direct attitude. She didn't want someone who was going to coddle her; she wanted someone who could help her figure herself out.

"Is that them?" she asked, pointing to a framed photograph of Charlie, a pretty redhead, and three kids—two redheaded boys and a brunette girl—of about ten.

"Savannah, Becker, Tate, and Ella." He beamed, his eyes sparkling as they rested on the picture. Then he pierced her with a sharp gaze. "Why are you here, Chloe? What do you need? I know that you lost your son ... you were five months pregnant at the time, right?"

"Yes."

"It was a car accident?"

She knew he knew the answer to that just as she knew he was trying to help ease her into telling him why she was there. "Yes. I was driving to work … it was pouring rain … I lost control of the car … slammed into a pole."

"You feel guilty."

He said it so simply.

Like he knew for a fact he was right.

Anger surged inside her.

Charlie Abbott had no right to say she was responsible for her son's death.

Chloe shot to her feet. "How dare you!" she screamed. "How dare you say it was my fault."

Hot tears blurred her vision.

That was not what she had been expecting the psychiatrist to say.

Why would he say that to her?

Why would he tell her that she had killed her son?

The tears came in a flood.

She dropped back into her chair and buried her face in her hands, sobbing hysterically for the second time tonight.

An arm wrapped around her shoulders, and although it was the doctor who had just accused her of causing her own child's death, she turned into him and wept into his chest.

Charlie said nothing, just held her and let her cry.

Eventually, her tears dried up, and she released her death grip on his shirt and straightened in her chair. "Sorry," she apologized, sniffling, embarrassed that she had just cried all over a stranger.

Charlie, on the other hand, looked completely unfazed, like people cried all over him every day. Perhaps they did. "I didn't say you were responsible for your baby's death," he said quietly. "I said it's what *you* think."

Guilt.

He was right.

She hadn't wanted to admit it, but he was right.

She blamed herself.

It was her fault.

She'd been driving, she'd lost control of the car, and as a result, her baby had died.

"I didn't know if I wanted him at first," she said quietly, fixing her gaze on her hands, ashamed to be admitting this out loud. "I even thought about ending my pregnancy. I'd just started at the FBI, and I didn't want to take time off or be relegated to a desk. I was being selfish. I even put him in danger because I didn't want him messing with the job I had dreamed about since I was ten. I let myself play bait knowing I was risking not just myself but my baby as well, and I ended up with a gun at my head. I didn't deserve him. And that's why I lost him."

Chloe expected Charlie to offer a string of platitudes, for him to tell her she was being silly, that of course, her son's death wasn't punishment for her selfish and careless attitudes.

Instead, he said nothing.

She chanced a look at him. "You agree? Losing him was my punishment for not wanting him to begin with?" Fresh tears brimmed in her eyes.

"Of course not." Charlie still crouched beside her chair. "But it doesn't matter what I think or what I know. *You* have to know it. You have to find a way to accept that what happened to your baby was a horrible tragedy but one that you are not responsible for. You can't spend the rest of your life punishing yourself for something over which you had no control."

Her head knew he was right, but her heart vehemently objected.

She hadn't wanted her own baby, then things changed, and she had, but she'd lost him anyway.

And the loss wasn't just hers.

It was Fin's, too.

She had taken his son from him, then crushed by guilt, she'd fled. Now, he hated her. She hated herself, too.

Chloe prayed Charlie could help her learn to forgive herself.

DECEMBER 21ST

8:50 A.M.

"How're you doing?" Tom asked as she set a cup of coffee down on his desk before dropping down into her chair.

Actually, all things considered, she was doing okay. Yes, things could be better. She could be looking forward to her first Christmas as a mom, and yes, she could have not made a fool out of herself with Fin yesterday, but she was feeling better after her visit with Charlie.

She liked Charlie Abbott.

A lot.

After she'd calmed down from her crying fit, she and Charlie had talked for hours. She had told him everything. Every single thing that had been going through her head when she realized she was going into labor and that at only twenty-one weeks her baby wouldn't survive, and everything that had gone through her head since.

For the first time, she had allowed herself to consider the possibility that what Charlie had said was right. That it wasn't her fault that her son had died. That even though she'd had mixed feelings when she'd first found out she was pregnant, that didn't mean she deserved to lose her baby. Chloe knew she would never have gone through with it anyway. She may not have liked the timing, but that wasn't the baby's fault, and she would never have terminated her pregnancy. Whether she had realized it at the time or not, she had already loved him.

She wasn't quite ready yet to admit that she wasn't responsible for her son's death, but now she could see that sometime in the future she might be able to believe it.

They had also talked a lot about her relationship with Fin and how her guilt at losing their baby had made her push him away. How could she look at him when she'd taken such a precious thing from him?

She still loved him, probably always would, and if he had given her even the tiniest indication that there was a chance for them—however slim—then she would have fought for them with every fiber of her being. But he had been very clear that it was over, and she had to respect that. Charlie had told her that things weren't always as they seemed, but in this instance, she was pretty sure they were. Fin hadn't been shy about telling her to leave him alone. So, she would.

Emotionally wrung out, she had fallen asleep as soon as her head hit the pillows and slept a deep and dreamless sleep. And when she woke up this morning, she actually felt better than she had in a long time.

Giving her partner a genuine smile, she pulled the reindeer beanie off her head and said, "I'm doing better. Thanks for yesterday." When he had found her crying in the office—which she was still embarrassed about. Being found by her partner in tears didn't really help her tough girl image—he had offered to call it quits for the day. She assumed in part it was so he could go home and check on his wife.

"I'm glad to hear that, and of course, you're welcome."

"Hannah feeling better?"

"She is." He nodded, and Chloe saw the relief in his face. Tom loved Hannah the way Fin used to love her. The kind of love where he would walk through flames, or search every corner of the globe, or rip to shreds with his bare hands anything that presented itself as a threat to her. Or anything else he had to do to make sure Hannah didn't get hurt.

She couldn't deny she was a little jealous.

Chloe hoped that one day she would find someone who loved

her like that.

"Want me to talk to Fin?" Tom asked. He had that protective look about him, and she fought back a smile.

She liked her partner and had learned a lot from him. When they'd first been paired up, she hadn't been sure how things would work out. Tom was so meticulous about everything. He noticed everything, and he used every little one of those details to help him decide on what the next and best move was in every case they worked. She just wanted to run in and catch the bad guys. Despite their differences, they got along great, and she hoped they remained partners for many years to come.

"Thanks, Tom, but that's okay. Fin's still angry. I get it. And he was very clear last night—it's over between us. That makes me sad, but I have to accept it. Otherwise I'm just going to wind up getting hurt. Right now, I have enough to focus on with work, friends, and family—there's plenty to keep me busy. And I think I need to spend some time working on myself; I have lots I have to work through and work out. Speaking of work, we have to figure out who The Breaker is."

Tom pulled out a few sheets of paper. "Hannah was pretty wiped out last night and went straight to sleep, so I did a little research."

"What did you find?" Chloe felt a little bad that her partner had been working last night while she had been talking to a shrink, but she had to accept that it was okay to take time out for herself sometimes. Not just okay, but necessary.

"The physical therapist that Fin told us about, Pete Larkin, he was right; there have been dozens of complaints against him by female patients."

"How does he still have a job, then?"

"Seems he moves around a lot, changes jobs frequently, and he comes from money, has a good lawyer. Although there are complaints, he's never had any criminal charges filed against him because he never did more than make the women feel uncomfortable with his questions and the way he watched them."

"So, he's creepy, but does that make him a killer?" They were looking for someone intelligent, and someone who had the means to be able to purchase equipment to help him with his bone breaking goals and to have a place to keep his victims for long periods of time without them being found. Pete Larkin definitely fulfilled the second, but was he smart enough to pull this off?

"He doesn't have a criminal record, and colleagues don't report that he's ever been anything other than professional, if not a little aloof, with them—which is part of the reason he's managed to never get fired."

"Why the obsession with broken bones? It's what he asks his female patients about, but why that specifically? It's not like everyone there would be there because of accidents; there would be stroke and seizure victims too."

"He was in a bad accident when he was a toddler. Fell off a third story balcony. Should have died, but somehow, he didn't. He broke over half the bones in his body, was in the hospital for over a year recovering."

Chloe nodded, digesting this. That could certainly explain the obsession with broken bones and could be where this idea to see if it was possible to break every bone in someone's body was possible. "What about Harley Zabkar?"

"I asked around about him before I left yesterday and Fin was right."

She refused to let herself think about Fin right now. The quicker she forgot about him, the better. "He doesn't get along with patients or colleagues?"

"No one likes him. He has zero people skills, but he is the best surgeon in the hospital. His IQ is off the charts. He graduated high school at the top of his class at the age of fifteen. He's performed surgery on patients no one else would even touch."

So that ticked the intelligence box. If someone could pull this off, then it would be someone like Harley Zabkar. "He got money?"

"Talk around the hospital is that he's deep in debt. He has a gambling problem, and apparently, he's into prostitutes; the real high-class ones."

"He have a connection to broken bones?"

"His sisters."

The way Tom said it piqued her interest. "What happened to his sisters?"

"He had two—one older, one younger. When he was seven, his parents were out, the kids were being watched by a girl down the street; she was seventeen. She invited her boyfriend over as soon as the parents left, basically left the kids to fend for themselves. An hour later, she hears a massive crash and finds four-year-old Helena at the bottom of the stairs. Harley was up top, claimed his sister tripped and fell."

"How badly was Helena hurt?" Chloe asked, sure she already knew the answer.

"Broken bones in both arms, both legs, a fracture in her skull, and broke her T1 vertebrae."

"She was left a paraplegic."

"She never said that her brother pushed her, but if he is the killer, then it's a reasonable conclusion."

"What about the other sister?"

"She fell off a cliff. She died."

"He pushed her."

"If he's our killer, then yes, most likely."

"He realized he needed to push them off something higher to break more bones," she said softly. The man was a sociopath. He didn't care about his victims. All he cared about was himself and what he wanted.

"Neither Pete nor Harley are married, so that would make it easier for them to keep a live victim for years at a time. Both have homes that are in the general vicinity where Taylor came from. Both fit the general description Taylor gave us."

"Both have a connection to broken bones, both have the privacy needed to commit the crimes. Harley Zabkar has the intelligence to pull this off, to keep the girls, to hurt them, and to leave behind no physical evidence. Pete Larkin has the financial resources needed to purchase the equipment Taylor told us about. So, which one is it?"

"What's your gut telling you?" Tom asked.

Chloe didn't even need to consider this, she knew which direction her gut was pointing her.

* * * * *

11:37 A.M.

Chloe hoped she was right about this.

She hadn't quite gotten to the point yet where she trusted her gut. She trusted it to tell her if something wasn't right and danger might be lurking close by, but she wasn't confident that it was competent enough to point her in the right direction. With time she was sure it would come, but lately, her self-confidence had taken a beating. Between the accident, losing the baby, and now Fin, she was doubting herself and her ability to know what the right thing to do was. But she would get through this, just like she had gotten through everything else life had thrown at her. And one day, she hoped she would be a great agent who was able to use every tool at her disposal including her gut instincts.

"Why do criminals always live in such normal looking houses?" she asked as Tom pulled up in front of a small brick colonial. The yard was a little overgrown but not excessively. There was no garage, and the driveway sat empty. It didn't look like Harley Zabkar was home.

"You think they should live in caves or dilapidated castles or something?" Tom asked with a small smirk.

"It would certainly make things easier," she quipped. "We

could just drive around and stop off at all the caves and dilapidated castles and pick them all up."

Her partner chuckled. "You're right—our job would be a breeze."

"This house is small and close to neighbors," she said, feeling a little dejected. She had wanted to be right about Harley Zabkar, but this didn't look like the kind of house where you could keep a young woman prisoner for years at a time. Surely someone would hear something, especially since they knew that he tortured his victims and broke their bones. There would no doubt be screaming, and neighbors would hear that.

"Doesn't mean it isn't him," Tom reminded her. "He could be our killer and keep his victims at another location."

"We didn't find any other property in his name."

"Doesn't mean he doesn't have any. Sometimes things aren't always as they seem." The second time in as many days that someone had said that to her. She knew that. But sometimes things *were* as they seemed.

"He's not here," she said as they climbed out of the car. It was just beginning to snow, and Chloe wished she could put her reindeer beanie on. To keep up her Christmas clothing quota, she was wearing her candy cane striped socks. They were thick and fuzzy and kept her usually cold feet toasty warm even on the iciest of winter days.

"Not that it looks like, at least," Tom agreed as they headed up the path to the front door.

"True." She rapped on the door. "He could be here, and his car just isn't, or it could be parked around the back."

There was no answer.

They waited a minute, then Tom knocked again, more firmly this time.

No footsteps sounded, but Chloe thought she heard a muffled cry. She glanced at her partner, whose face had creased as he tilted his head toward the door. "You heard that, right?"

"I did."

"Someone is in there."

"Sounds like it."

"I don't think its Harley Zabkar." As she said the words, Chloe could feel adrenalin flood her system. They may have not only found the killer but also Avery Ormont. In minutes, they could have their guy in custody, and his victim saved. *This* was exactly why she had joined the FBI. "We have to go in."

Tom nodded and reached for the door handle. It didn't turn.

"Break the door down," she said, anxious to get inside. Avery needed them, she could already be hurt. They'd heard something inside there, and since they suspected this man was the serial killer they were looking for, they had probable cause to get inside however they could.

Tom peered through the glass panes in the door then carefully broke one, reaching inside and unlocking the door. Once it was open, they both pulled out their weapons and stepped inside.

The foyer was large. A dining room was to the left, a lounge room opened to the right, and beyond that, she could see a kitchen. There was a staircase in front of them leading up to the first floor.

She was just about to suggest they split up—Tom could take downstairs, she'd take upstairs—when someone suddenly growled and launched at her.

Startled, she stumbled backward. A scream almost tumbled from her lips, but she managed to hold it back. FBI agents did *not* scream at potential crime scenes.

Wait.

It wasn't some*one* who had launched at her.

It was some*thing*.

A cat, to be exact.

It meowed irritably at them and darted out the still open front door.

The stupid cat had nearly given her a heart attack. It had come out of nowhere. One second the room was empty, and the next it was there, clearly unhappy about being left cooped up inside the house.

"It's not funny," she snapped at her partner who was laughing at her.

"You should have seen your face," Tom managed to get out through his chuckles.

"You wouldn't have thought it was so funny if it flung itself at you. Cats are dangerous, you know; I still have the scars from the one we had when I was a kid." Cats were not her favorite animal; she was definitely a dog person. Fin, on the other hand, had been a cat guy, and she had been forced to cohabitate with his psychotic black cat. The thing would go from peacefully sleeping to trying to shred your skin with its sharp claws in less than a second.

"The cat was what we heard," Tom said, sobering. "There isn't anyone in here. That means our probable cause to search the house is gone."

Chloe shrugged. "We just say we didn't find the cat till we'd already searched the house." He looked at her warily, so she added, "There's no way to know for sure that it was the cat crying to be let out that was the sound we heard. Remember, things aren't always as they seem." She threw his words back at him.

Still looking a little hesitant, Tom nodded his assent. "All right, let's check the rest of the house, make sure there isn't anyone being held here against their will. You take upstairs, I'll do down here."

She took off up the stairs and checked out the three bedrooms and two bathrooms that were up here. The two guest bedrooms contained nothing more than beds. The master had clothes everywhere. Apparently, on top of the reported gambling addiction, Harley was also addicted to shopping. The master bath was messy but not excessively so, and the other bathroom was completely empty.

There was no one up here.

And nowhere she could see where you could stash a victim.

"Hey!" a voice yelled out downstairs.

Not her partner's voice.

"FBI, Mr. Zabkar," Tom informed him. "Please—"

Her partner was cut off by a weapon firing.

Chloe was already on the stairs by then, running down them. "Put the weapon, down, Mr. Zabkar," she ordered.

When he saw her, he paused for a moment, and she thought he was going to shoot at her too. But he didn't. Instead, he turned and fled.

She ran straight to her partner.

He was standing, leaning back against the wall clutching at his leg.

Which was coated in blood.

"Tom?"

"It's nothing, a flesh wound. Go after him," her partner said. His face was tight with pain, but his eyes were clear, his voice strong, and his color good.

Leaving him to call in backup, Chloe grabbed the keys he held out and dashed outside in time to see a car take off up the street, tires screeching.

She was in the car and following him by the time he rounded the corner.

She called in her location and the description of the car.

She had her sirens going, and she had caught up to him, following close behind, but he was refusing to pull over.

He had to know he wasn't getting away—other police cars were coming, and he'd be boxed in and forced to stop. He may as well just do it now and get it over with.

They had just rounded another corner when he accelerated, putting a little distance between them. Before she could speed up, he had hung a U-turn and was heading straight for her.

He'd obviously floored the gas; he was coming at her quicker.

He wasn't stopping.

They were going to collide.

At the last minute, Chloe turned the wheel sharply, avoiding crashing into Harley Zabkar's car, but placing her directly in line with a pole.

She didn't have time to swerve.

A major sense of déjà vu filled her. This was just like the day she had lost her son.

A moment later, her car hit the pole with a bone-shuddering thunk.

Her body was slammed into the steering wheel, then yanked back by the seat belt.

Pain swallowed her up, and she sank into the blackness.

*****

12:21 P.M.

"Are you coming back?" Taylor watched him anxiously.

"I'll stop by to say goodnight at the end of my shift before I go home," Fin told her. When he'd come into her room last night, she had calmed instantly. Her family hadn't been thrilled about that, and to be honest, he wasn't either. He didn't want to be the only thing that calmed Taylor down.

She, however, seemed thrilled with how things had worked out. She'd chatted away with him while she ate some dinner, all but ignoring her parents to focus her attention on him. Once she'd eaten, it'd taken some persuasion to convince her to lie down in bed, close her eyes, and try to go back to sleep. Eventually, she'd complied and had fallen asleep almost instantaneously.

As soon as Taylor fell asleep, he said a quick goodnight to her family and made a hasty retreat. Fin was uncomfortable with Taylor's attachment to him. They were strangers, although she'd told him her entire life story along with every like and dislike that she had so he felt like he had known her forever. He was trying to do the right thing, but it was still awkward.

"Can't you stay?" Taylor's large green eyes begged.

"No, I need to go home, and I have some errands to run." Being firm was important. He couldn't give in to Taylor's every demand. She had to accept the idea that he wasn't a part of her life. He was just the guy who found her. He wasn't going to be around forever.

"Well, could you just stay until I fall asleep?" she tried. She was certainly persistent.

"Dr. Patrick has things to do, honey," Taylor's mother said gently.

Taylor ignored her. "Please," she wheedled. "I'm afraid to go to sleep. What if I have nightmares again?"

"Your family is here if you need them," he reminded her.

"But—"

Taylor was interrupted when Eric Abbott threw the door open. "Fin, I need to talk to you. Now."

Something was wrong.

Very wrong.

Fin could see it on his friend's face.

Fear flowed through him, just as it had the day of Chloe's accident. He'd just arrived at the hospital when some cop who had been the first to arrive at the scene of the car crash had called him—on Chloe's instruction—to tell him that she had been hurt. He had wanted to go running straight to the scene, but the cop had said an ambulance was already coming and would bring Chloe to the hospital.

Seeing her, with blood streaking one side of her face, her arm splinted, and bruises already appearing all over her body, had virtually stopped his heart. He hadn't known until he helped pull her stretcher out of the back of the ambulance that she was already in labor.

Then his heart *had* stopped.

He had known immediately that there was no way the baby could survive. He had just prayed that Chloe would.

That day had been the worst of his life.

That feeling of helplessness, and pain—the kind of pain that no amount of morphine or painkillers could take away—still lingered. He doubted it would ever go away.

Without saying goodbye to Taylor, he hurried from the room. "What's wrong?" he asked as soon as Eric closed the door behind them.

"Don't panic," Eric started.

"Don't panic," he repeated. The only time someone ever said that was when they had really horrible news. "How bad is it?"

"It's Chloe."

It felt like the world stopped. Everything froze.

His heart stopped beating; his lungs stopped breathing; his blood stopped flowing through his veins.

Something had happened to Chloe?

Something couldn't happen to Chloe.

It was impossible.

Was she dead?

The thought ripped out his soul.

He couldn't imagine a world without her in it.

How could she die thinking that he hated her?

How could he live knowing the last time they'd been together, he had treated her so badly?

There had to be a mistake.

"Fin, she's not dead. I said don't panic," Eric snapped him out of his panic before he could completely lose it.

"What happened to her?" he asked tightly. Why didn't Eric just spit it out? The longer he took, the more terrifying scenarios his mind concocted.

"She was in a car accident."

Another car accident? "How badly is she hurt?"

"Apparently, she was unconscious when first responders arrived, but she's awake and talking now."

"Where is she?"

"You can't go running off down there."

In answer, he just turned and started for the door. He would search every inch of the city if he had to, but he would find her.

"Wait, what about Taylor?" Eric came after him.

"What about her? I was leaving anyway, and this is Chloe."

"I thought it was over between you two."

Fin just glared. It might be over between them, but that didn't mean he didn't still love her. "Where. Is. She?"

Eric sighed but rattled off an address.

As soon as he had it, he was off. He ignored Eric's calls for him to stop and listen.

He didn't want to stop and listen.

He didn't remember getting out his keys or climbing into his car or turning on the ignition. The next thing he knew, he was just driving as fast as he could.

His stomach was twisting and twirling, tying itself in knots. His hands were shaking so badly he could hardly keep control of the car.

He had to see Chloe.

The need consumed him; it was all he could think about. He had no idea how many stop signs he ignored or how many red lights he ran or what speed he was going.

Nor did he care.

All he cared about was getting to Chloe.

What if she was more seriously injured than Eric had let on? His friend had said she'd been unconscious. She could have serious head injuries—not to mention injuries to her spinal cord or internal injuries. What if she had injuries she couldn't recover from?

The police cars, fire truck, and ambulance signaled that he had arrived.

Stopping the car vaguely close to the side of the road, he jumped out, not bothering to turn the engine off or close his door.

Fin frantically scanned the crowd.

Where was she?

The ambulance was empty.

He could see the car she'd crashed; it was scrunched up against a pole. It was also empty.

Fin was about to have a fear induced nervous breakdown when he spotted her.

She was standing under a tree, and it looked like she was arguing with someone.

She looked fine.

His fear turned to anger. Was this just some crazy stunt to pay him back for treating her badly last night?

Furious, he stalked over to her but froze a couple of feet away.

Blood streaked her face just as it had after the last accident. Her shoulders were hunched, and she held a hand to her chest as though it caused her pain. Although she was arguing with an EMT, her voice was weak and raspy.

He must have gasped aloud because she suddenly turned toward him, her beautiful brown eyes grew wide with surprise, then narrowed in suspicion. "Fin, what are you doing here?"

"What do you think?"

The blank look she gave him said she genuinely had no idea. "I don't know. Last night you were very clear that you wanted nothing more to do with me."

He really wished he had a comeback for that, but he didn't. She was right. He'd been awful to her, and she had no reason to believe that he still cared about her. "Angry doesn't mean I don't love you anymore," he said quietly.

Chloe's pale face was shocked, and she rubbed at her eyes as though she thought she might have just imagined what he'd said.

Before she could say something, he started toward her. "I need to check you out."

She held up a hand to stop him. "I'm okay. You don't need to."

"She wouldn't let us examine her," the EMT inserted.

"I am looking you over, Chloe. Don't even think about arguing. I just about had a heart attack when I heard what happened. You were knocked out … you need to be checked out."

Fin gently grasped the hand she held out between them and led her to his car. She stumbled a little, struggling to keep her balance, and he worried that she had a concussion. Chloe didn't offer any more protestations, but he wasn't sure if that was because she was okay with him looking after her or because she felt too bad and was in too much pain to bother arguing.

Struggling to keep his composure, he forced himself to slide into doctor mode. Doctor mode was safe. He didn't have to worry about his feelings, which were quickly welling up toward overwhelming.

"How long were you unconscious?" he asked as he helped her sit in the back seat of his car.

"I don't know—a few minutes, maybe," she replied, resting her head back against the headrest.

"You have a headache? What about dizziness and nausea?" He reached into the front and pulled a penlight from his glove box.

"A little of both," she admitted.

"Let me look." When he took hold of her chin and tilted her face in his direction, her eyes met his, and she sucked in an uncertain breath. Her lips parted, and the tip of her tongue darted out to wet them. Her breath was warm as it puffed against his cheeks.

Vulnerability bloomed in her eyes, and he knew he was being unfair to her. He shouldn't have treated her like he had last night, and he shouldn't be here right now. He was being selfish. He was here because *he* had needed to see her, but he hadn't considered if this was what was best for her. She was vulnerable right now, and he felt like he was taking advantage.

"You need to go to the hospital," he said a little breathily. Being this close to Chloe, it was hard not to kiss her, to tangle his fingers in her soft brown locks and run his hands all over her perfectly toned body. But he couldn't. She was hurt, and they weren't together. It wasn't his place to touch her like that anymore. Fin had to remind himself why it was they had broken up in the first place, or he was going to throw all his doubts to the wind and accept her invitation to dinner, providing it still stood.

"I don't want to go to the hospital. That's what I was arguing with the EMT about when you showed up."

Why was he not surprised about that? He would have argued with her about it, but he knew why she didn't want to go to the hospital. The accident would have brought up all those feelings and emotions from that day. Everything was too fresh. She couldn't handle the hospital right now, and he didn't have the heart nor the will to force her. And this way, he got to spend a little extra time around her.

"You probably have a concussion, and that cut needs stitches."

"You can do that though, right? Or the EMT?"

"I can," he confirmed, shining a light in her eyes. Her pupils were equal and reactive. Setting the light down, he picked up her wrist and checked her pulse. It was a little fast but nothing drastic, no doubt a result of the shock and trauma of the accident. She'd had her shoulders hunched earlier, so he suspected her ribs had taken a battering but needed to be sure. "Where else are you hurt?"

For a second, it looked like she was debating not telling him, but then she relented. "The airbag didn't deploy. I hit the steering wheel pretty hard. My chest hurts a little bit."

He raised a skeptical brow. "A *little* bit?"

Chloe rolled her eyes. "Okay, more than a little, but I don't think they're broken."

Attempting to keep as much professional detachment in place as he could muster, Fin placed his hands on Chloe's chest and immediately knew that any chance of professional detachment was out the window. His mind may still be angry at his ex, but his body clearly hadn't gotten the memo. It responded instantly to the feel of her soft breasts beneath his hands.

"Uh, how does that feel?" he asked, hoping Chloe didn't notice the sudden change in his demeanor.

"It hurts, but really, it's not so bad."

"Probably just bruised or cracked then, not broken. What else?"

"My stomach is a little sore from the seat belt," she admitted.

Easing up the hem of her sweater, he immediately saw a nasty black and blue bruise forming. He probed her stomach, ignoring the now uncomfortable throbbing between his legs. She winced at his touch, but she didn't seem to be in too much pain, and her vitals were stable, so it was likely just bruised.

She'd been lucky.

She could have been killed.

Instead, she had walked away with relatively minor injuries.

"He was coming right at me," she murmured, her eyes going distant and glazed over. "He wasn't stopping. I didn't have a choice. I had to swerve out of his way. The pole was coming too quickly. I couldn't miss it."

Tears began to roll slowly down her pale cheeks, mixing with the blood that still covered her face, and she started to tremble.

Don't do it, he warned himself.

Don't touch her.

Don't comfort her.

It's only going to make everything worse.

Despite what he told himself, his arms curled around Chloe and drew her against his chest. He inhaled her scent, absorbing the feel of her body so close to his, he allowed his heart rate to pick up. Fin knew that he wasn't angry with her anymore.

* * * * *

3:00 P.M.

She couldn't stop shaking.

Her worst nightmare was coming true.

Hannah Drake jumped out of her car—she may or may not have turned off the engine first—and ran up her drive. She reached into her bag for her keys but couldn't seem to find them. In a panic, she began tossing things on the ground as she searched through her too big purse for them.

Finally, she located them.

The next problem was her hands were trembling so badly, she couldn't slide the key into the lock.

After several failed attempts, she was pretty much ready to find a rock, toss it through the nearest window, and climb through it to get inside.

Then somehow, the door opened.

"Hannah?"

She froze.

Her eyes slowly moved to the man in the doorway.

It was Tom.

Her husband was standing there in one piece, but it had to be a trick.

She hadn't been feeling well the last few days, but this morning she'd gone into work. There was a big meeting with a new client who wanted to sell their jewelry in her store, and she hadn't wanted to reschedule. She'd had her phone off because she didn't want any interruptions as she negotiated the best deal she could.

Besides, she hadn't been worried about anyone needing her during those couple of hours.

She had been wrong.

When her newest client left, and she finally turned her phone back on, there had been almost four dozen messages and missed calls.

All of them had been about Tom.

Apparently, her husband had been shot.

She hadn't bothered listening to much more information than that. Just left her employees to finish out the day and lock up and jumped in her car.

While she had expected to go to the hospital, probably to find Tom lying hooked up to a ventilator in a bed in intensive care, the messages had instead directed her to head home.

The entire drive she had been expecting to be met by a family member or a colleague of Tom's or both. She'd thought they were going to sit her down and gently inform her that her husband had been killed in the line of duty. Tom had been shot. If there was no need to go to the hospital, that had to be because he was dead, right?

So why was he standing there looking the same as he had when they'd both left for work this morning?

It had to be wrong.

It *had* to be.

Hannah shook her head.

No.

This was wrong.

She must be hallucinating.

Or maybe this was Tom's ghost.

She didn't believe in ghosts, but what else could it be? If he had been shot, then he couldn't be standing here looking fine.

"Hannah."

Ghost Tom or hallucination Tom or whoever he was took a step toward her, and she quickly backed up.

"Hannah, it's all right. I'm okay. Really."

She just shook her head at him.

She knew what guns did.

It was why she was deathly, paralyzingly afraid of them. She had tried so hard to overcome her phobia, but so far, she hadn't had a whole lot of success.

"Hannah, calm down." Tom was speaking to her slowly, a look of concern on his face. Why was he concerned about her? He was the one who had been shot. "You look like you're going to pass out. Come and sit down."

She was still backing up, but he quickly advanced on her and wrapped warm, strong hands around her biceps.

Hannah drew in a shocked breath.

He felt real.

He felt alive.

Her knees buckled, but before she could crumple, she was being swung up into Tom's arms. He carried her inside easily, even pausing to balance her in one arm while he scooped up the contents of her bag. He wasn't walking like he was in pain—had she imagined the whole phone call thing?

In the living room, he set her down on the sofa and squatted in front of her. If she hadn't seen the small grimace, she really would have believed the whole thing had been a figment of her imagination.

"Are you okay?" he asked.

"Me?" she asked—or possibly screeched. She would have been more embarrassed about her meltdown, but she had already been running on empty and then finding out Tom had been shot and driving here in a panicked blur had her at the end of her rope. "Are *you* okay? I thought you were shot." Her eyes were roaming his body, searching for his wound.

"It was just a flesh wound," he assured her, reaching out to hold her, but she swatted his hands away.

"Where?" she demanded.

"Really, Hannah, I promise, it's nothing. Just a scratch."

"Where?" she repeated. She wasn't going to be coddled and kept in the dark.

"My leg. But the bullet just skimmed me. It didn't even need stitches."

Hannah stopped listening after the word *leg*. Instead, she scrambled to her feet, dragging Tom up with her and began to unbuckle his belt, tossing it aside and sliding his pants down his legs.

When she saw the bandage wrapped around his left thigh, she dropped down to her knees.

Her husband had been shot.

The word echoed in her head.

She could have lost him.

What if the bullet had hit his inner thigh instead of his outer thigh? Then instead of just skimming across his flesh, it might have nicked his femoral artery, and he could have bled out before help ever arrived.

"You keep that up, and I'm going to have you naked upstairs in bed before you can blink," Tom said wryly. His eyes were on her hands which were convulsively rubbing his leg above the top of the crisp white bandage.

She glanced up and saw that his body was clearly interested in what was about the last thing on her mind right now. He was such a man. "How can you even be thinking about sex after you were just shot?" she asked as tears began to well up in her eyes, spilling out onto her cheeks.

"Because I'm really okay and I have a very beautiful wife." He took hold of her hands and drew her up to her feet, wrapping an arm around her waist and settling her against his chest.

"Tom, what happened?" she asked as another shudder rippled through her body.

He tightened his hold on her, one hand stroking the length of her spine, the other settled against the back of her head, rubbing small circles. "Chloe and I were at the house of a suspect. We thought we heard cries for help inside, so we broke in. Once we got inside, we found out it was only a cat. We were checking out the house anyway just to be safe when the man returned. I identified myself as FBI, but he pulled out a weapon and shot at me. Then he went running off. Chloe followed him, but he tried to ram her car with his, and she ended up crashing."

"Is she okay?"

"Yes."

"And you're sure *you're* okay?"

"Positive," he assured her, pressing his lips to the top of her head.

His assurances did little to calm her wildly thumping heart. "I'm sorry. I shouldn't be crying all over you. *You* were the one who was shot." She sniffled and tried to get control of herself. She wasn't usually such a mess, but anything to do with guns—especially guns in conjunction with her husband—made her lose her mind a little. She really was going to have to try to get a handle on her phobia.

"Shh, don't be sorry," he soothed, catching her tears on his thumb and brushing them away. "I'm sorry you were scared. I wanted to go to the store right away so you could see for yourself that I was fine, but my leg was a little sore to try driving."

"You should be keeping off it," she said, pushing him down onto the sofa, ready to descend into full-on fussing mode. But Tom hooked an arm around her waist and brought her down with him, laying her on top of his body. "I'll hurt you," she protested.

Tom just chuckled. Despite the brave front he was putting up for her benefit, she knew he must have been scared. The thought of anything taking him away from her and leaving her on her own would have terrified him.

"I love you, Hannah," he whispered, his breath warm against the side of her face.

"I love you, too," she whispered back, tilting her head up so she could press a kiss to the side of his jaw.

At the touch of her lips, she felt Tom settle, the stress and anxiety melting from his system. Hannah let it melt from hers, as well. Her husband was okay, and while she knew he had a dangerous job, and there was always going to be a chance that something could happen to him, she couldn't let herself obsess over that. If she did, she would never be able to function.

Letting her lips trail a line of kisses along his jawline then up to his lips, she needed to feel closer to her husband. She needed something to calm her frazzled nerves. She needed an affirmation of life.

There was only one thing she wanted to do right now. Maybe it wasn't such a guy thing after all. "Want to go upstairs?"

* * * * *

6:48 P.M.

"Don't get out of the car, I'll come 'round and help you."

Chloe just looked at Fin in shock. She was completely confused by his behavior over the last twenty-four hours. She'd been caught off guard by his hostility when she had tried to make peace with him and see if they could get back together. Then she'd been caught off guard when he had showed up at the scene of the accident—he was the last person she had been expecting to come. Next, he'd caught her off guard by holding her so gently in his arms when she had cried.

Now he was catching her off guard by insisting that he bring her home from the hospital.

She hadn't wanted to go to the hospital, but somehow Fin had managed to get her there. She wasn't quite sure exactly how he had managed it. One minute she'd been in the back seat of his car, crying on his shoulder, and the next she was being scooped up into strong familiar arms and carried through the ER doors.

Fin had reluctantly allowed another doctor to examine her, and when he had insisted that she go for x-rays of her chest and scans of her head, she had agreed. Not because she wanted to. What she wanted was to get as far away from the hospital and all its horrible memories as quickly as possible. But Fin looked so concerned, and she knew the only thing that would ease his worries was to have the tests done.

They had come back fine. No concussion, no broken ribs, no internal bleeding. She was just battered and bruised, emotionally as well as physically.

When she'd been discharged, she had been about ready to call her parents or her brother, to come and get her, but Fin had been most insistent that he would take her home.

She didn't know what to make of him.

Talk about giving her whiplash. Going from hating her to telling her that he still loved her.

Chloe had no idea what to make of that.

Did that mean he actually did want to fix things between them, but he was still too angry with her to actually do it?

Did it mean that he had just been scared?

Did it mean that they had been together for years and a part of him would always feel something for her?

She was so confused.

"Take it slowly," Fin cautioned as he opened her door, unbuckled her seat belt despite the fact she was more than capable of doing it herself and took hold of her elbow.

His touch was so gentle.

The look in his eyes so tender.

Why was he doing this to her?

Couldn't he just tell her what was going on inside that head of his?

Carefully, she swung her legs out of the car; she was sore all over, and even the tiniest of movements started up the dull ache that consumed her.

Her legs wobbled as she stood on them. They weren't quite steady enough to hold her up yet, still stuck firmly in the jell-o phase. She swayed, and probably would have face-planted into the sidewalk if it weren't for Fin's firm grip on her elbow.

He led her up the path and to her front door, where he produced the key—she guessed he must have gotten it from her bag which he had clutched in his free hand—and guided her inside.

There he floundered a little.

When she'd left, he had kept the house they had lived in together, and she had stayed with her brother for a couple of weeks before finding her own house to rent. Fin had never been here, so he didn't know where to go.

"Family room and kitchen are down the back," she said.

Fin gave a brisk nod, then began to lead her down there. Chloe didn't think she was going to make it. She hurt all over; her heart worst of all. What had happened today was way too close for comfort to what had happened seven months ago.

Right now, the physical pain was dwarfing the emotional pain, but she knew that wouldn't last indefinitely.

Sooner or later the pain that was steadily building up inside her was going to come bursting out.

She was a little afraid of what would happen when it did.

Sucking her bottom lip in, she tried to keep her focus on just putting one foot in front of the other. She didn't remember hurting this badly after the last car accident. Although that was probably because she'd had bigger problems at the time than her own discomfort.

A pitiful moan very nearly slipped out despite her efforts to hold it back. She didn't want to worry Fin more than he already was.

While she hadn't known that he still cared, it was nice to know that he did, and she didn't want to take advantage. Chloe was sure he was struggling with memories of the day their son died just as she was. Maybe she should have insisted on calling her brother to come and get her.

Had her house grown since she'd left it to go to work this morning?

It didn't usually take this long to walk from the front door down to the family room.

Fin muttered something under his breath, and then the next thing she knew her feet were being lifted off the floor, and she was being carried through the house. She fought against it, but instinct had her arm curling around his shoulders and her head nestling against his neck.

This wasn't a good idea.

She didn't know where Fin stood yet.

She couldn't allow herself to start dreaming about a fairy tale ending for them.

If nothing else, they had dated, and she had been the mother of his child. It made sense that he cared about her, might always care about her, and still have lingering feelings.

But that *didn't* mean he had changed his mind from what he'd told her last night.

He might still want nothing to do with her.

He might still be furiously angry with her, but his concern had temporarily pushed it aside.

She couldn't let herself hope until she knew for sure where Fin stood and what he wanted.

"You should have just asked me to help you," he said as he set her down on the sofa.

"I thought I could make it." Chloe searched his eyes, trying to find in them the answers she sought.

"How are you feeling?"

"Sore." She tried to shrug but quickly realized that was a bad idea.

"How's your vision? Blurry? Seeing double?"

"It's fine."

"Still dizzy?"

"A little."

"Nauseous?"

"No." Fin slipped so easily into the doctor role. Caring and yet detached. Maybe she was misreading things. Her thoughts were too jumbled up to make sense right now.

"I'll get you some painkillers."

Chloe wondered briefly how he was going to find them, but apparently, the hospital must have given her a prescription, because Fin pulled a small bottle from his pocket, unscrewed the cap and tipped some into his hand. Then he went into her kitchen, rummaged through cupboards until he found a glass and filled it with water.

"Thanks," she said when he brought them to her. She was too tired and too sore to protest taking them. Anything that would make her feel better was okay with her.

When she was done, Fin took the glass and set it on the coffee table in front of the sofa he'd set her down on.

Now what?

She felt awkward around him. Unsure what to say or do because she wasn't sure what was going on behind Fin's impossibly impassive face.

She wished he would do something.

Anything.

Yell at her, talk to her, kiss her.

The last one caught her a little by surprise.

Under the circumstances, kissing her ex should be the last thing on her mind. But it wasn't. It was *exactly* what she wished he would do.

Chloe sighed.

Having Fin here like this wasn't helping. She just wanted to go to bed, go to sleep, and wake up in the morning as though none of this had ever happened.

"Where are the instructions the doctor left for taking care of the stitches?" she asked. Thank goodness Fin had been paying attention to her follow-up care instructions because she had been too spaced out to listen.

"Don't worry about it; I'll look at it in the morning."

"Wait. What?" she asked, confused. "Are you going to stop by on your way to work?"

"No. I'm staying here tonight."

What? "You're staying here tonight?"

"You were knocked unconscious, you should be monitored overnight. I thought you knew I was staying. I told the hospital; that's why they didn't admit you."

Fin was staying with her.

It was exactly what she wanted, and yet the look on Fin's face was not what she wanted to see. She wanted him to *want* to stay with her, not stay out of some sense of obligation. And right now, he didn't look particularly enamored with the idea of spending the night.

She mustered a smile for him. "You don't have to stay, Fin. I'll be fine. I can ask my brother to come and stay if you're going to worry."

"Chloe." It was all he said, but the emotion in his voice conveyed everything she needed to know.

Fin *did* still love her.

He *did* still care about her, and not just in a "she's my ex" sort of way.

He wasn't angry with her anymore.

He still wanted her.

"You should get some rest. Unless you're hungry and want to eat first," Fin said, back to being all business.

She curled her nose at the thought of food, but the thought of bed was tantalizing. Of course, bed with Fin in it would be even better, but she knew neither of them was there yet.

"I think I'd rather go to sleep."

Fin nodded, and before she could even begin to motivate her body to assume a standing position, he had picked her up and was heading for the stairs. Chloe snuggled close. She and Fin may not be back together, but they were certainly one step closer to getting there.

DECEMBER 22ND

6:47 A.M.

Chloe had hoped that when she woke up this morning, she would be feeling a whole lot better, but as soon as she stretched and pain billowed out from her chest, radiating out to every inch of her body, she realized that wasn't going to be the case.

She didn't care, though.

Fin was here, and he still loved her.

There was hope for them.

She knew she would have to fight for them and that was fine with her. It was her fault, after all, that they were stuck in this mess, so it seemed only right that she work hard to fix what she had broken.

Waking up knowing that Fin was in the house with her gave her a kind of peace she hadn't felt in so long. It was nice. Not being alone. Chloe had her friends and her family, but it wasn't the same. She missed having a partner. She missed having someone there when she went to bed each night and when she woke up in the morning. She missed having someone to talk about her day with. She missed having someone to watch TV with in the evenings or go out to dinner with or go out with on the weekends.

She missed being in a relationship.

She wished she had never walked away, even if at the time it had felt like the only thing she could do. She had blamed herself for the baby's death—she'd been gutted inside. Not only had she not done her job and carried her child safely to term, but she had deprived Fin of his son. Every time she looked into his devastated eyes and saw how much pain he was in, it was like another piece of her died. Guilt was killing her. If she had stayed, she wouldn't have survived.

Chloe knew she should have sought help earlier. At the time, the hospital had offered to set her up with a counselor, but she hadn't wanted to. Everything was too raw; she couldn't talk about it. Even now it was hard, but she also knew that it was necessary.

Despite the mistakes she had made, fate had been kind to her.

Now she had a chance to get it all back. Maybe one day she and Fin would even have another child together.

Excited to see him, she dragged her bruised body out of bed and headed to the bathroom. Last night when Fin had carried her up to bed, she had been too tired to really get a good look at the damage done in the accident. Although it'd only been seven o'clock, she had just stripped off her clothes, left them in a pile on the floor, tossed on the oversized sweater she slept in and dropped into bed. She didn't even remember Fin turning off the light.

He must have taken her dirty clothes with him. How sweet was that? Fin loved doing laundry; he'd do it pretty much every day. She, on the other hand, hated it. It was her least favorite chore, and she usually procrastinated and put it off until she was out of clean clothes and had no choice.

Gingerly, she lifted the sweater, gasping as she saw the mottled mess of black and blue and purple that was her chest and stomach. The combination of the seat belt and the steering wheel had really done a number on her.

Her head didn't look much better. The small cut had been neatly stitched and covered with a white square bandage. Bruises peeked out from underneath it, spreading up and down her forehead, and heading for her cheek. She was going to look a mess for her mother's annual family photo on Christmas day.

Still, she was lucky she hadn't been hurt worse. The defective airbag could have gotten her killed.

Quickly, Chloe brushed her teeth, ran a brush through her tangled hair, held the washcloth under the hot water then washed her face, carefully avoiding her injury.

Feeling much more human, she pulled on a pair of sweatpants and stuck her feet into her Christmas tree slipper boots and headed downstairs. Although she knew nothing was going to make her look good right now, she did want to look as good as she could for Fin.

She knew he would be up. He had always been an early riser, so it was no surprise to find him in her kitchen cooking breakfast.

"Morning," she said as she stood at the bottom of the stairs.

"Morning," he said as he turned to give her an examining look. His gaze settled on her slippers, and she saw a small smile tilt his lips up. It had been such a long time since she had seen him smile. She'd missed that most of all.

Her crazy Christmas clothes had always made him laugh, and although she had been into it since she was a child, it had sort of become a tradition she shared with Fin. He was always on the lookout for something to get for her, and sometimes, if she was lucky, she could convince him to wear a pair of Christmassy socks or even some Christmas boxers.

"I did your laundry," he announced, turning back to the stove.

"Thank you."

Chloe couldn't move.

All she could do was stand and stare at Fin. He looked good even in the same clothes he'd been wearing the day before. His hair was a little longer than he'd had it when they were together, and he was sporting just the right amount of scruffy stubble to look sexy.

Even though they had been together for years, she still got that feeling of butterflies in her tummy when she saw him. Her heart pitter-pattered, and her hands got sweaty. She wanted to feel his lips crushed against hers, feel his hands teasing her body and working it into a frenzy, then she wanted him inside her.

She was stupid to think she could walk away from Fin and that would be that.

How could she ever love another man the way she loved him?

No matter how much time passed or how many days, weeks, months, or years they spent apart, nothing was going to diminish their love.

She couldn't wait a second longer.

She crossed the family room. Fin turned and opened his mouth to say something, but whatever it was got cut off when she kissed him.

Chloe had a picture in her head of how this would play out. She would kiss Fin, he'd wrap an arm around her waist and drag her closer. His tongue would find its way between her lips. He would pick her up without ever breaking the kiss and carry her upstairs to bed. They'd rip off their clothes and get reacquainted with each other's bodies. They would drive each other wild with their hands and their mouths, and then when neither of them could take it any longer, they would make love.

But that wasn't what happened.

Fin's hands curled around her shoulders, and he pushed her away. "What do you think you're doing?" he demanded. His dark blue eyes weren't full of lust or love or anything closer. They were full of anger.

Anger?

What was going on?

Yesterday he'd told her that he still loved her. He'd taken her to the hospital, then back to her place. He'd spent the night and even done her laundry. He was cooking her breakfast.

"I ... I ... I thought ..." she stuttered.

"You thought what?" Fin growled. "That you could kiss me? We're not a couple anymore. I told you that."

Tears of embarrassment, hurt, and anger filled her eyes. "But you said you still loved me."

"I also told you that I didn't want us to get back together."

At least he didn't deny that he still loved her.

That meant something. Right?

What was she thinking? Chloe growled at herself.

Why was she letting him treat her this way?

They had both lost a child. Yes, guilt had made her walk away, but surely Fin had to understand that that was all it was. She knew he had abandonment issues, but that didn't give him the right to take his anger out on her.

She had to wake up.

If it was over, she had to stop living in fairy tale land.

In the real world, there wasn't always a happily ever after.

Yes, she loved Fin.

Yes, she probably always would.

But this was crazy.

She couldn't keep doing this. She couldn't keep holding out hope that they could work things out when Fin kept making it clear that it wasn't what he wanted.

However, if he didn't want to be together, then he had to stop with the mixed signals.

It wasn't fair.

If he wanted to channel anger because it was easier than being hurt, then she could do that too. "Get out."

"I can't," he said with infuriating calm. "I have to check your wound, make sure there are no signs of infection."

Hell would freeze over before she let him touch her again. "Yeah, that's not going to happen."

"I also want to make sure that you eat something," he continued as though she hadn't spoken. He even had the gall to turn back to the stove and start dishing up eggs onto a plate.

"I am not eating breakfast," she said tightly. Who did Fin think he was? He didn't want to be her boyfriend, but he wanted to be her mother.

"Are you feeling nauseous?" Fin asked sharply.

"Get out, now," was all she said, trying really hard not to let it come out as a hysterical shriek.

"I'm going to be checking on your head every day until the stitches come out, so you better get used to that idea." He watched her like he was daring her to disagree.

"That is not happening. No way. So, *you* get used to *that* idea. Now, get out of my house." The last word did come out a little hysterically shrieky.

She didn't have to put up with this.

Charlie had told her that she didn't have to let her guilt rule her. She didn't have to take Fin's anger. It wasn't the punishment that she deserved like her guilt kept trying to convince her it was. She knew all of that, of course, but somehow having someone else say it to her made it seem more real.

She must have muttered something under her breath because Fin frowned at her. "Charlie Abbott? What about him? Are you seeing my friend's brother? Personally or professionally?"

For someone who had just turned her down flat, he seemed awfully interested in her life all of a sudden.

Since he had made no move to go anywhere, Chloe decided if he wouldn't leave, then she would. She spun on her heel and ran for the stairs.

She hoped she could make it into the shower before the tears came.

* * * * *

9:03 A.M.

Avery woke to a blinding pain in her hand.

It was so bad she was surprised she had been able to fall asleep.

Not that her sleep had been all that restful. The pain had somehow followed her in, haunting her dreams and keeping her tossing and turning on her fluffy mattress.

Her tormentor had been true to his word. No matter how she had begged and pleaded, he had given her nothing to ease her pain. Her thumb still had a lump in it where one end of the broken bone had been displaced. He said he had no intention of fixing the beak so that it would be a constant reminder of the consequences of disobeying and angering him.

Part of her hadn't thought he was serious when he told her he would leave her to suffer if she didn't do what he said.

That was stupid of her.

This was hell. She couldn't live like this indefinitely. She was going to have to give him what he wanted.

What he wanted was an apology and an acknowledgment that he was the one in control here. That he had had all the power.

It would kill her to say those words, but the alternative was way worse.

How would she cope when he broke her next bone?

If just this one little break was this bad, then what would it be like when he moved on to a bigger bone? At least at the moment, she could still move about, go to the bathroom, eat, but what about when he moved on to a leg? Without painkillers and crutches, how would she get about? Would he continue with his punishments and make her wet the bed rather than help her get to the bathroom, or even give her a catheter? How would she cope with the pain of multiple broken bones?

As much as she hated to admit it, Avery wasn't sure she could.

The cumulative effect was going to be the stuff of nightmares.

She needed painkillers.

It simply boiled down to that.

And if the only way to get them was to play along, then she would have to swallow her pride and do it.

Avery sat up, careful to use only her good hand, keeping her other cradled protectively against her chest. She couldn't afford to jostle it. Even the slightest movement sent sharp bolts of agony darting up and down her entire body.

Maybe she could splint it herself?

It might make him angry, but at least it would help to clear her head a little. If she couldn't focus and think, then she was never getting out of here. There had to be a way to escape. She couldn't allow herself to think otherwise, and if she was going to find it, then she had to be able to concentrate.

Walking slowly so as not to move her hand, she went to the toilet and did her business. Since he hadn't given her any underwear, just a new clean white cotton dress each day, she was able to get things done without causing herself too much additional pain.

There wasn't a lot in the room that was moveable, she thought as she scanned the room. It was mostly just the furniture, and there was no way she was going to be able to break something to get a piece of it to use to make a splint. But there wasn't really anything else. Although he brought her food and wanted to make sure that physically she was as strong as possible so her body could withstand the trauma he intended to put it through, he obviously wasn't as interested in her mental health. There was nothing to do here. No TV or computer or phone—not even some books to read.

He had given her a few toiletries, though.

Maybe there was something she could use there.

She had a toothbrush, a hairbrush, a washcloth, and a single piece of soap.

The soap and the washcloth were useless. The hairbrush was too bulky. But the toothbrush might work. She'd hate not being able to brush her teeth, that little piece of normalcy stopped her from completely feeling like a trapped animal in a cage, but who knew how long she'd be able to keep doing it anyway. Eventually, she was going to wind up bed bound and unable to get about. If giving up brushing her teeth saved her a bit of pain by splinting her broken thumb, then it was worth it.

Avery was searching for something to use to secure her broken digit to the firm handle of the toothbrush when she heard the unmistakable sound of the door opening.

He was back.

With a meal or to hurt her again?

She almost couldn't bring herself to turn around, preferring to hover in blissful ignorance and hope for a little longer.

"Good morning, Avery."

He always sounded so calm and conversational. She hated that. He should sound like the insane lunatic he really was. It was only fair.

She drew in a deep breath.

It was now or never.

The longer she put this off, the harder it was going to be.

Although this was going to be one of the hardest things she thought she would ever have to do, she knew she had to do it. She had weighed up the pros and cons, and this was the decision she had made.

Avery turned around and dropped down to her knees. The jolt sent pain arrowing through her body, but she did her best to ignore it. Keeping her gaze fixed firmly on the man's feet, she didn't think she could do this if she looked him in the face. She didn't want to see him looking all smug when he realized he had broken her this quickly. She had thought she would be able to fight for as long as it took. Turned out she couldn't be more wrong. One broken bone and she was such a quivering mess she was willing to sell her soul to the devil just to get some painkillers.

"I'm sorry for disobeying you," she said quietly. "I'm sorry that I tried to escape. I'm sorry that I wasn't grateful for your offer of morphine and treatment for my broken bones. I won't do it again. From now on I will be respectful and obedient and appreciative of the things you've given me. Please forgive me." Her voice wobbled a little on the last word, but she'd done it. She'd said it. Now she just had to pray that it worked. That he bought it. That she could outwardly be the meek, compliant girl he wanted, all the while plotting her escape in her head.

The wait for him to respond felt like an eternity.

Avery saw his feet move closer. Each footstep rang with an air of finality.

He hadn't bought it.

She knew it.

He was never going to ease up on her. He was going to keep breaking her bones without anesthetic and morphine, without him setting the breaks. He was going to torture her, and it was just going to keep getting worse and worse until her body gave up and she died.

A sob was about to come bursting out when a gentle head rested on her head. It caressed her tenderly as though in some weird way he actually cared about her.

Then he said the words she'd been longing to hear. "You're forgiven. Your punishment is over."

Avery slumped in relief and couldn't help but let out a whimper as her injured hand bumped into the floor.

The man knelt in front of her. He reached out and picked up her hand, examining her thumb. "I think you learned your lesson. Would you like me to fix this for you?"

"Yes," she said immediately. Right about now the possibility of being out of pain was the most wonderful thing she could think of.

"Yes, what?" he prompted.

"Yes, please." For a deranged killer, he certainly had a thing for manners.

"Yes, please, who?"

Master? Sir? Boss? What did he want her to call him? He had never specified that he expected her to address him as anything specific. Avery supposed he really didn't care so long as the name denoted the fact that he was in charge here. She settled on one she could stomach. "Yes, please, sir."

He nodded approvingly, then took her elbow and helped her

stand, guiding her to sit at the table. "Let's get some painkillers in you and then I'll set your hand. After that, you can have some breakfast; you're going to need your strength for later today. I think it might have been a mistake to wait for so long in between sessions. I think the key to making this work is to keep moving. One break every forty-eight hours. Don't worry, though—you keep doing as you're told, and I'll make sure we manage your pain."

With that, he retrieved a medical kit that was kept in a locked cupboard then joined her at the table. Her whole body was trembling at the knowledge that soon her pain would float away into nothingness. She could barely process what he'd just told her. All she could focus on were the painkillers that would soon be working their way through her system and dulling her pain.

"Avery."

His tone had gone very serious, so she tore her eyes away from the bottle of pills and looked at him.

"Don't challenge me again. If you do, I promise you that you will not like the consequences."

With that threat hanging in the air, he finally gave her the pills.

She prayed she had made the right choice and that this was what was going to keep her alive until help arrived or she found a way to escape.

* * * * *

1:31 P.M.

"How are you doing?"

"Fine," Chloe replied shortly.

"Are you sure?"

"Tom," she exploded. "Stop asking me that. You're driving me crazy."

"Just concerned about you," her partner replied calmly,

unfazed by her outburst.

Chloe sighed. She knew he was. She'd been edgy and tense all morning, definitely not giving off the impression that she was handling things at all well. Maybe she should have taken the day off like the doctor at the emergency room last night had recommended. Although she knew if she'd done that, all she would have done was spent the day moping around and attempting to let go of her irritation toward Fin.

At least this time she had gotten the message.

She hoped.

Surely, she wouldn't be stupid enough to hold out hope of reconciliation after the way he had treated her this morning.

Maybe she had been a little slow to catch on at first, but now she got it. There was no hope for them. Fin might still love her, but that didn't mean he was interested in rekindling anything.

It was time to move on.

It was time to say goodbye to the past and finally look to the future.

Maybe after the hoopla of the holiday season quieted down, she'd even start looking for someone new to share her life with. She wanted to be happy. If Fin wanted to live in anger holding on to the mistakes she had made and what she had cost him, then that was his choice. But she wanted to be happy.

"You should go home."

"*You* should go home," she snapped at her partner. She knew he was just trying to show he cared but he was driving her crazy with the constant inquisitions—he'd been at it all day, ever since they'd met in the elevator. "You're the one who was shot."

"A scratch," he corrected.

"Is that how Hannah saw it?"

"No. She freaked out. Just like Fin did."

Chloe shook her head. "It's over between Fin and me. I mean, *really* over. And I'm finally ready to accept it. I don't have to take his anger. I know I hurt him by leaving, but I have finally accepted that I don't have to keep punishing myself by letting him take his anger out on me."

"Of course, you don't," Tom sounded indignant. "You didn't do anything wrong, Chloe. Sometimes when something really bad happens, and it feels like guilt is going to crush you, you need some space. Fin could have asked you to stay. He could have fought for you. He needs time to process the loss just like you did. Give him some time, and he might come around."

"He's had time."

"It took three years for Hannah and I to find our way back to each other."

"That was different," she protested.

"How?"

Chloe just shrugged. She would love to believe that given enough time Fin would come around, but she couldn't spend her whole life waiting to see if he would. What if he never did? "I don't think Fin and I are going to get the same happy ending that you and Hannah did."

"Okay. Well, whatever you decide to do, I just want to see you happy." Tom reached across their desks and patted her hand.

"Thanks." She smiled at him. Tom was a good guy, and she was glad that he had gotten the woman he loved back. "Is he waiting for us?"

"Yes, interview room three."

"You ready?"

"Ready." Tom's brown eyes glowed with anger. He hated anything that hurt Hannah, and Harley Zabkar's actions yesterday had hurt her. Tom would do whatever it took to make sure the man was charged and imprisoned for what he'd done, and if Harley was also the serial killer, then he would make sure he went down for that, too.

Just as she was getting up, her phone rang. No name popped up on the screen. She was going to leave it, assuming it was a marketing call or something, but snatched it up at the last minute.

"Hello?"

"Chloe Luckman?" The female voice on the other end of the line was unfamiliar.

"Yes." Uncertainty settled in her belly, making her feel faintly nauseous.

"This is a call to inform you that Marcus King has been released on parole."

The bottom dropped out of her world.

Marcus King.

Out.

He was supposed to be serving a life sentence.

How could he be getting out?

And why hadn't she been notified that there was a parole hearing?

If she'd known, she would have been there and made sure that man never saw the light of day.

How could this be happening?

And on top of everything that had gone on the last few days.

This was the last thing she needed.

"Chloe?"

She blinked, and Tom's concerned face came into view. He had taken the phone from her hand and presumably disconnected the call since her phone now sat on her desk.

"Who was that?"

"Marcus King," was all she could get out. Her tongue seemed to have swollen to ten times its normal size, and her lips seemed to have gone numb, making speech difficult.

Tom's forehead creased. "What about him?"

"Parole."

"Parole?" he echoed incredulously. "How did that man get parole?"

"I don't know."

"I'm so sorry. Do you want to go home?"

Home?

No.

Not at all.

It was the last thing she wanted.

What she wanted—needed—was to do something to equalize her world out. She was feeling completely out of control with the accident and Fin, and now learning that Marcus King was a free man. She needed to take back some of that control. She needed to make sure that Harley Zabkar was punished, and if he was the serial killer, Tom wouldn't be the only one who would do whatever it took to make sure he never spent another day as a free man.

"Let's go do this interview."

Before her partner could argue, she was heading straight for the interview room.

She didn't wait for Tom before opening the door and walking in. "Good afternoon, Mr. Zabkar."

The man who sat looking back at her was in his mid-thirties, had large, long-lashed green eyes, and wavy dark hair. He was good-looking, and he knew it. Arrogance was rolling off him in waves and filling the room.

He thought he had them beat.

He didn't think he would ever see a day inside a prison cell.

He thought he was smarter than them and that he was going to win.

He was wrong.

"Good afternoon, agents." Harley shot them a sickeningly sweet smile.

Tom closed the door, and they both went to sit opposite Harley and his lawyer. He watched them calmly, completely unruffled by being asked to come down to the FBI offices. He didn't care that less than twenty-four hours ago he had shot her partner then run her off the road. How he thought he was going to get away with it, she didn't know. All she did know was that she wouldn't let him.

"You are being charged with two counts of attempted murder of a federal agent," Tom's voice was just as calm and unruffled as Harley's face, but Chloe could feel her partner's anger.

"I didn't know you were FBI agents." Harley leaned back in his chair and crossed his legs. He might be good-looking, but his clothes and shoes were cheap. Maybe the rumors about his gambling addictions were true.

"I identified myself," Tom said.

"After I fired my weapon. Which I have a concealed carry permit for," he added.

"No, Special Agent Drake identified himself as an FBI agent *before* you fired your gun," Chloe contradicted. She was sure Tom had. She'd heard her partner speak, then the gunshot as she was coming down the stairs.

Harley shrugged. "Maybe I missed that. I came home to find a strange man in my house. I assumed you were there to collect on a debt. I may have gotten myself into a little trouble with some gambling, and I took a loan from a loan shark. I know I shouldn't have, but I was desperate. I didn't have the money to pay them back, and I thought you were there to make good on the threats. I was just defending myself." He said it with sincere earnestness in his voice, but his eyes gave him away. He didn't care. This was all just a game to him. A game he thought his superior intelligence was going to help him win.

"Then why did you run?" she asked.

"You came down the stairs. I thought you had been sent by the loan shark as well. He wasn't clear exactly how many people he would send after me or what they would do if I didn't come up with the money."

"You aimed your car at me, ran me off the road."

"You were following me. I was defending myself."

Harley Zabkar must have waited for the crime scene unit to finish up at his house yesterday before returning home because he had been picked up there this morning. Obviously, he wasn't so afraid of these supposed people who were coming after him because of an unpaid loan to return home where they would find him.

"You were in my house illegally. Why would I not have thought you weren't there for nefarious reasons?" Harley asked all wide-eyed innocence.

"We came to ask you some questions about a case and thought we heard cries for help coming from inside," Tom said.

"I didn't know that at the time," Harley said smoothly.

"Do you know a young woman by the name of Taylor Sallow?" Tom asked.

"No. Should I?"

Although she searched his face for any signs of deceit or anxiety or fear, she saw none.

"She was a victim of a serial killer. A serial killer who likes to kidnap women and break their bones," Tom said.

"I *fix* people's broken bones," Harley reminded them. "And I'm very good at what I do."

"We'll be bringing her in to do a lineup," Chloe told him. "She'll be able to identify you."

Harley looked bored. "No, she won't. Look, I'm sorry you were hurt, agents, but that wasn't my fault. And I won't be doing any time for it. You have no proof I did anything wrong. I defended myself, plain and simple."

He said it like that was case closed.

But this case was far from closed.

And when it was, he would be facing spending the rest of his life in prison.

* * * * *

2:08 P.M.

This was the last thing he wanted to be doing today.

Especially after that disaster of a morning.

Fin was an idiot.

Chloe had kissed him, and he had pushed her away and then hurt her again.

What was wrong with him?

He hadn't really meant to do it. She just caught him by surprise. She'd come downstairs looking ridiculously sexy in those stupid Christmas tree slippers. And then she'd kissed him. He wasn't ready for it. He had panicked. Not because the kiss wasn't good, but because he didn't think he could just kiss her and be done with it.

If they kissed, they would wind up in bed, and that wasn't what he wanted.

Was it?

He really didn't know anymore.

Chloe had mentioned Charlie and that she didn't have to take his anger. It wasn't that he disagreed with her. He knew he was treating her unfairly; he just couldn't stop.

But he wanted to.

For the first time since their son died, he didn't *want* to be angry with Chloe.

If she was seeking professional help, was that his fault? Had he pushed her too far? Had he been too mean, too selfish, too cruel?

He wanted to apologize, but a simple sorry didn't seem like enough. How could he make up for the way he had treated her?

He didn't deserve her forgiveness.

He had taken out his grief and anger and helplessness on her at a time when she had needed him. He hadn't been there for her. He had turned his back on the woman he loved when she had needed him the most, and he was ashamed of it.

Fin had been planning on asking her to marry him. From the second she told him she was pregnant, he'd known that she was the only woman for him. Well, he'd known it long before then, but that was the moment he decided he wanted to make it official.

He'd bought the ring, intended to propose after the birth of their child.

Only, then the baby died, and everything had gotten so messed up that he was no longer sure it was possible to put all the pieces back together again.

He had failed the two people it was his job to protect.

Chloe's accident was his fault.

He should have driven her that day. He usually did when it rained since Chloe didn't particularly like driving in wet conditions. But he'd been busy. Anxious to get to work for some reason he could no longer even remember.

Because of his selfishness, she had lost control of the car and crashed it.

Because of his selfishness, his son had died.

All this time when he'd been angry with Chloe, he was really just angry with himself.

Her heart had broken when their baby died, and he had done that to her. How could he forgive himself for that?

Fin needed time to think.

Chloe wanted to get back together, and he didn't know what he wanted. When she had first walked away, it had seemed like a blessing in disguise. She knew his past and how many other people had walked away from him, and yet she'd done it anyway. That had given him the perfect outlet for all the anger that was building inside him. Being angry with Chloe certainly beat being angry at himself.

But he couldn't lie anymore.

Not to Chloe and not to himself.

He just wasn't ready to face her yet.

"Thanks for coming with me." Taylor reached for his hand and tried to entwine their fingers as they walked through the halls of the FBI building.

"Yeah, sure."

He hadn't wanted to come with her, but when Tom had called

and asked for Taylor to come down and identify a suspect, she had begged and cried and pleaded until he caved and agreed to come. Eric had played the guilt trip thing again, and although her family was in the car waiting to take her home afterward, he was the one coming inside with her.

At least she was going home now. Physically, she was growing stronger, and her broken leg was healing well, so there was no reason for her to be in the hospital any longer. Fin hoped that now that she would be at home with her parents, she wouldn't feel like she needed him anymore. He had enough to worry about with Chloe without being the only one who calmed Taylor down.

"Fin."

He turned and saw Tom waving at him. Chloe was standing behind her partner and the look on her face when she saw him was anything but pleased. Trying to apologize to her was going to be even harder than he'd thought.

"Thanks for coming down here," Tom said to him and Taylor when they joined the agents.

"Did you catch him?" Taylor asked timidly.

"We think so, but he's denying everything, so we need you to see if you can pick him out of a lineup," Tom explained.

"I'll have to see him?" Taylor panicked, her fingernails digging into his hand as she clutched at him.

"Yes, but he won't be able to see you. It's one-way glass; you can see him, but he can't see you," Tom assured her. "I'll go see if everything is set up."

Once Tom left, Fin took a tentative step toward Chloe, shaking off Taylor's hand as he went. "Chloe," he began hesitantly.

She just glared at him and turned her back, fiddling with papers on her desk.

She was angry.

That was fine; he deserved that.

She'd gone out on a limb and took a huge risk admitting that she still loved him and that she wanted to get back together. He'd told her he still loved her, too, but that had been driven by fear. Now it was time to take the same risk she had.

"Chloe, I'm sorry about this morning."

She said nothing.

She wouldn't even turn to look at him.

"I shouldn't have been so harsh with you. It was wrong," he babbled helplessly. He wasn't good at apologizing, even when he knew he was in the wrong and knew he had to.

She still refused to say anything.

Instead, she just turned and stalked off.

"Don't take that personally," Tom said from behind him. "She had a bit of a shock earlier."

Panic suddenly flared inside him.

Had something happened?

Was she more seriously hurt from the car accident than they had thought?

"What happened?" he demanded.

"I think it's up to her to decide if she tells you or not."

"Don't give me that," he growled. "What happened?"

Tom sighed. "Marcus King is out on parole."

That was the last thing Fin had expected to hear.

How could that man get out after what he'd done?

Why hadn't she told him?

She said she wanted to get back together and yet every time something important happened, the first thing she did was walk away. How could he ever trust her if she kept doing this? If she loved him and wanted to be with him like she claimed, then she had to stop running from him. She had to tell him when she needed him; she had to turn to him. She had to give him the chance to be there for her.

Leaving Taylor with Tom, he headed off after Chloe. She was going to talk to him whether she liked it or not. Finding out that man was out there must be terrifying.

He found her staring aimlessly into a cup of coffee in the corridor.

"Tom told me about Marcus King," he said quietly as he came up behind her.

"He shouldn't have done that," she muttered.

Gently, he took hold of her elbow and turned her to face him. Her bruises had grown darker in the few hours since he'd last seen her. Although she tried to hide it, he could see the fear lurking deep in her brown eyes. She didn't want to be afraid, but she was. Why wouldn't she be? That man was a monster.

"Why didn't *you* tell me?" Sure, they had their problems, but she knew he loved her, so why hadn't she told him about Marcus King?

"Why would I?" Anger wiped away some of the fear in her face. "You have made it *very* clear that you are no longer interested in me. I get that you still have lingering feelings, we both do, but you said it's over and I accept that. That means my life is no longer your concern. Marcus King, my injuries from the accident—neither of those has anything to do with you. We're not together. You got what you wanted, so let it go. Let me go. You can't have it both ways."

Fin hated that she was right.

"We have a problem," Tom announced, joining them.

"What?" Chloe asked.

"Harley is out on bail."

"What?" Chloe said again, this time shocked.

"He's still claiming that he didn't know we were FBI agents when he shot at me and drove his car at you."

"You identified yourself," Chloe said.

"I know, and we'll prove that when this gets to court. But we have no evidence that he's The Breaker—"

"That's why Taylor is here," Chloe interrupted, clearly frustrated.

"I know, but somehow his lawyer got him out already. Harley

Zabkar is free until this goes to court or we get some evidence."

"What?" Taylor's shrill voice demanded.

* * * * *

2:27 P.M.

Did she hear that right?

Taylor was sure she must have misheard.

Did the FBI agents really just say that the man they thought had kidnapped her, held her prisoner for nineteen months and broke her bones was still out there?

But they'd had him.

That's why she was here so she could identify him, and they could officially charge him with the crimes.

Only, now he wasn't here.

They had lost him.

What was wrong with them?

Weren't they the FBI?

Wasn't catching bad guys their job?

So, why had he left?

The pretty brunette. Special Agent Chloe Luckman. *She* had to be the reason that the man who had hurt her had gotten away. Because the stupid woman wanted Fin.

But Fin was hers now.

And it was the agent's job to catch the man who hurt her, but she'd been too busy scheming and plotting to get back a man who didn't belong to her to do her job.

That was unacceptable.

A rage unlike anything she had ever felt before ignited inside her.

It started in her chest and it grew and grew. She could feel it moving throughout each part of her body. Consuming her. The agents and Fin were talking to her; she could see their mouths moving, but she couldn't hear the words. She didn't care about the words.

There was only one thing she cared about right now.

One person was standing between her and happiness and peace.

Agent Luckman.

The woman was getting in between her and Fin, and she was responsible for the man who hurt her not being safely in prison.

Taylor wanted to kill her.

She had never been a violent person. She'd never felt this kind of rage before—but nineteen months as a captive of a crazy, violent psychopath who liked to break things had changed her.

With a near inhuman howl, she leaped at the older woman.

None of them had been expecting her to do something like that and she managed to connect with Agent Luckman, knocking her to the ground.

She had lost it.

She didn't really know what she was doing.

All she knew was that she had to get the fear and pain and anger out of her.

And the only way to do that was to kill the person responsible.

Since she couldn't get her hands on her kidnapper, this woman would have to do.

She swung her fists; she scratched with her nails; she kicked with her feet. She did everything she could to inflict the maximum pain in the shortest amount of time.

Someone was yelling at her—she guessed to tell her to stop, but she was beyond listening. She was beyond the real world now. Existing only in a dark, empty, hollow place filled with desperation.

An arm hooked around her waist, and she was dragged backward.

She shrieked like she'd lost her mind, and maybe she had, but she wasn't finished with the woman, and now she was being pulled away from her.

"Taylor, stop. Stop." The second stop was accompanied by a sharp shake that seemed to snap her back into reality.

Fin had ahold of her, and Agent Drake was kneeling beside his partner. Agent Luckman's hair was a mess, her shirt was torn, and her face and arms were streaked with blood.

Had she really done all of that?

Her anger disappeared instantly, like a flame that had been doused with a bucket of water.

In its place was despair and shame and more fear than she could cope with.

The man was still out there; he could come back for her. She was never going to be safe as long as he was alive.

"What were you thinking?" Fin asked. He sounded angry. She had alienated the one person who kept her feeling marginally safe.

"It's her fault!" she screeched. "Her fault that he got away."

"No, it isn't."

He was looking at her like she had lost her mind.

She probably had.

"Tom, is she okay?" Fin asked.

"She's fine," the woman answered for herself, clambering to her feet with the aid of her partner.

"You're bleeding," Fin stated the obvious.

"I said I was fine," Agent Luckman snapped.

"Let me take a look at you." His grip on Taylor began to loosen, and jealousy speared her, reigniting her burning rage. Why did he have to care about his stupid ex? It wasn't even like they were still together. If he released his hold on her, she was going to fling herself right back at her target.

"You stay with Taylor," Agent Drake ordered. "You need to calm her down, and she's not going to listen to anyone else. I'll take care of Chloe."

"I'm fine," the woman insisted once again.

"She needs to see a doctor," Fin said.

"I'll make sure she's taken care of. Just take Taylor into one of the interview rooms and calm her down."

As Agent Drake led his partner away, Fin dragged Taylor through the crowd that had gathered to watch what was going on and into a small, quiet room. Taylor suspected that if she hadn't been a victim of such a heinous crime, then she would be in handcuffs right about now.

She didn't care in the least.

They could put her in handcuffs if they wanted. They could cart her off to jail and lock her up in a cell. She didn't care.

She didn't care about anything anymore.

"Why would you do that? Chloe is doing everything she can to find the man who hurt you. She was almost killed trying to stop him."

Taylor just shrugged.

"This behavior is unacceptable."

He was talking to her now like she was some spoiled, recalcitrant child. Although she supposed that was how she was acting.

"You have to understand that there isn't anything between us. I found you, I know that I make you feel safe, I know that you need to feel that way right now. But this obsession you have with me, it's just a coping mechanism."

How dare he downplay her feelings, make out like she didn't know what was going on inside her own head.

"They're not!" she screamed. "I love you. And if you would just forget about *her*, then I know you would love me too. It's her fault. She let him get away, and now she's stealing you away from me."

"No, honey." His voice turned impossibly soft and gentle, and he grasped her upper arms in his strong hands. He gave her a sad smile, then he reached out and tucked a stray lock of hair behind her ear, took hold of her chin and tilted her face up, so she had to meet his gaze. "You and I are not together. We are never going to be together. I care about you and your future. I want you to recover. I want you to be happy. I want you to be able to do everything with your life that you want to. But not with me. I think it's my fault. I've given you mixed signals by always being here. That ends today. You're going to go home with your family, and you're going to let them help you. I know what you went through was horrendous, and I know that it messed with your head. But let them help you. They love you."

And he didn't.

She could see it in his eyes.

He was with her physically, but his mind and his heart were still with Chloe Luckman.

This was really it.

The end.

After this, she was never going to see him again.

What would happen to her?

How would she cope?

What would she do when she was afraid if she couldn't have Fin close by?

Her family didn't understand.

They weren't there.

Taylor didn't think she could do it. She didn't think that she could let Fin go. There had to be a way to keep him. To convince him that she needed him, that she couldn't survive without him.

But as she looked at him, she knew there wasn't.

She had lost him.

Chloe had won, and she had lost.

Anger and jealousy spent, the tears came next.

They came in a deluge, bursting out and flooding down her face in a relentless stream.

She wasn't doing it on purpose to try and emotionally blackmail him. She already knew that it would do no good.

Taylor tried to stop them, but she couldn't.

She wanted Fin to wrap his arms around her and hold her

against that sturdy chest, letting his heartbeat soothe her until her tears finally dried up.

But he didn't.

He patted her awkwardly on the shoulder and waited for her to gather herself, his mind still with his ex. He wanted to go to her, to make sure she was okay, he didn't want to be stuck here with her.

It was time.

Time to climb out of the little protective bubble she had created for herself. She had to face the real world. She was free. She had her whole life ahead of her, she had to find a way to make it work.

On her own.

Without Fin.

With more strength than she thought she had, she straightened her spine, sniffed away the last of her tears, and prepared to let go of the first man she had ever loved.

* * * * *

7:43 P.M.

Chloe stood staring at her Christmas tree, her Spotify Christmas playlist singing in the background, and a candy cane in her mouth.

This time last year her world had seemed so perfect. She had been pregnant with her first child, and she had finally realized that she was excited about the prospect of becoming a mother, even if it meant taking a little time away from the job she had dreamed about having most of her life. She and Fin had been so happy, and she'd had an inkling that he might even be thinking about proposing.

Everything had been perfect.

And now …

Now, she had nothing.

She wandered over to the box she kept squirreled away in the back of her closet. This evening when she got home from work tired and sore, she had pulled it out and brought it down to the family room. She only ever got it out when she was feeling particularly reminiscent.

And when she was feeling like a good cry.

Right about now, she needed a good cry.

A cleansing cry.

Chloe put her candy cane on a coaster, knowing it would leave a sticky mess behind that she would have to clean later, but at that moment, she didn't care. She sat down on the sofa and set the box on her lap, opening it slowly, and staring inside.

One by one, she began to remove the contents.

The first thing she took out was a snowman Christmas tree decoration. Written in blue cursive script, it said, "Baby's First Christmas." She had bought it in the after Christmas sales. It and about a dozen other cute baby's first Christmas decorations. She couldn't make up her mind which one she liked best, so she had bought them all. She'd had to get all of them in blue and pink since it had been too early on in her pregnancy to find out if they were having a boy or a girl.

This year she had considered putting one of them on the tree in memory of her son, but she hadn't been able to make herself do it.

Maybe it would be good for her.

Maybe it would be a gentle reminder of her son, a special thing to do each year to keep his memory alive. She didn't ever want to forget him. He might have only lived a few minutes, but he would forever be a part of her.

Taking the snowman with her, she stood and crossed to her tree. It was smaller than the one she and Fin had because she'd left that one behind at their old place when she left. That one had been nine feet tall, barely fitting in their living room. This one was six feet tall, and just the perfect size for her living space.

As well as a new tree, she bought new lights and tinsel but had retrieved the special decorations from her childhood from Fin's house. They made the tree feel like hers, and even though she wasn't full of her usual Christmas spirit this year, the tree made her feel more normal. Like she was at least pretending to move on with her life.

Choosing pride of place right in the front, she hung the snowman.

It looked perfect.

While she would never hold her baby in her arms as she hung his special ornament or watch him do it himself when he got old enough, and then look at it on his own tree when he grew up, every time she put it on, she would think of him.

Her beautiful baby would live on in her memories.

A single tear trailed down her cheek.

Chloe returned to the box and began to unpack the rest of the contents. Besides the ornaments, there were several little baby Christmas outfits. She hadn't just gone overboard buying decorations; she had done it with the clothes too. There were several little onesies, a reindeer, a snowman, a Santa, a candy cane, a Christmas tree, and an elf. There were matching booties and baby mittens, there were beanies—including a little reindeer beanie just like the one she always wore.

She had been so excited to dress him in these adorable little outfits.

She couldn't part with them, and she wasn't sure she would be able to dress any future children she may have in them.

They were Christopher's.

Chris.

That's what she'd secretly been hoping to name the baby, although she and Fin had never finalized their choice of names.

Chris would forever be a tiny baby, and all of these baby things would forever remain his.

Although her eyes burned, tears wouldn't come tonight.

She was too tired.

Mentally, emotionally, and physically.

The last few months, especially the last few days, had taken their toll on her.

Her body ached worse than it had this morning after her scuffle with Taylor Sallow. The poor woman was struggling. She knew what that was like. She could have pressed charges, but what would be the point?

So, she had a few scratches on her chest and arms, and the stitches in her forehead had been ripped open. That was nothing compared to what Taylor was going through.

She just wanted the woman to get the help she needed.

Even if that help was Fin.

There was no point in being jealous of Fin helping Taylor. She and Fin weren't going to get back together, so she had to get used to the idea of him with another woman.

Besides, she had bigger things to worry about right now than Taylor. Or Fin, for that matter.

Marcus King.

It was hard to believe he was really a free man now.

It felt surreal.

She had never thought this day would come.

He had threatened to come after her if he were ever released.

She was the one responsible for putting him behind bars.

Chloe had been ten when she'd met him. She had been walking home from a friend's house. It was only down the block from her house, and she had whined continuously about having one of her parents come and collect her. She was ten years old, surely old enough to make the short walk home by herself.

It'd been summer, and nearly nine at night. It was getting dark, but the last lingering rays made it light enough to still see fairly easily.

She'd walked only a few houses along when she'd spotted the

car.

A big white van.

It had started moving when she closed the gate at the end of the garden path of her friend's house.

Only it didn't take off normally and drive off down the street.

Instead, it trailed along slowly.

Following her.

She knew instinctively that it was bad news.

The man had pulled over, rolled down his window, and called out to her. Asking for help finding an address.

He had looked normal enough, but the swirling feeling in her stomach had told her he wasn't normal.

She had screamed at the top of her lungs, startling the man and he'd quickly driven off.

People had come, and she'd told what had happened. The cops had turned up—and the FBI. She had gotten a good look at the man and remembered part of his license plate number. They were able to find him, and it turned out that he was responsible for the rape and murder of at least four other little girls in the neighborhood.

It was her testimony that had helped put him away.

And in court, on the day he was sentenced, he had screamed threats at her.

But he had been given life, so how was he out on parole?

It didn't make sense.

Chloe didn't really think he was a threat to her. Sixteen years had passed, and she was no longer a helpless little girl. Now she was an adult, an FBI agent; she was armed, and she knew how to protect herself. She wasn't really worried, but she was a little uneasy.

On the couch beside her, her phone began to buzz.

It was Fin.

Again.

This had to be the twentieth time he'd called her.

Couldn't he take a hint? She hadn't answered any of his calls. Surely, he could see that meant she didn't want to talk to him. If he was worried about whether Taylor had hurt her, he could always get an update from Tom. And if he wanted information on the Marcus King case, he could get that from Tom too—not that her partner knew any more than she did about it.

A gigantic yawn nearly split her face in two.

She was tired.

It was only eight, but she may as well go to bed.

Before she did, there was one more thing in the box that she had to take care of. Christopher's stocking.

She lifted it out of the box. It was gold and had Santa, an elf, and a reindeer standing in front of a Christmas tree. She had intended to have his name embroidered on the top after he was born. She'd also bought a matching stocking hanger. If she'd put the ornament on the tree, she may as well go all the way and put his stocking up too.

Chloe took it to the mantle and set it up beside her own.

She might not have anyone else in her life right now, but she would always have her son.

DECEMBER 23ᴿᴰ

10:13 A.M.

"Are you sure you should be up and about and not home in bed?" Savannah asked her friend.

"Positive," Chloe replied. "Really; it looks worse than it feels."

"That doesn't really convince me—it looks pretty bad, so I'm sure you feel worse than you're letting on."

She was pretty sure that her friend was lying. Chloe had to be in a fair bit of pain, she just didn't want anyone to know it.

Savannah knew all about that.

It had been close to three years since she'd been hurt, and her hip still caused her pain. Most days it wasn't so bad, a little twinge here and there if she took the stairs too quickly or turned too sharply. When the weather was frigid, she tended to get more pain, and her joint would seize up. Some days it would be so bad it was all she could do to keep the tears at bay until she got home

But in the big scheme of things, it wasn't her ruined hip that hurt the most.

It was her broken heart.

Broken bones were a lot easier to heal—even if they didn't heal completely correctly—than a broken heart was.

She shook off the doom and gloom. She had a lot to be thankful for. She had a job she adored, even if it wasn't the one she had originally wanted. She had a wonderful family and great friends who had supported her every step of the way during her long recovery. And it was Christmastime. She loved Christmas, especially all the baking. She usually started on December 1ˢᵗ and baked something new every day. Fudge, cookies, cakes, pies; she had so much stuff, she was always giving most of it away as it was way too much for one person to eat.

On Christmas Eve, her baking efforts culminated in baking and assembling a huge gingerbread house. She usually went with a theme; she'd done the traditional Christmassy things at first: Santa's house at the North Pole, the Nativity, but then she decided to start being original. She had done her childhood home and family, the FBI with all her colleagues, and a few of the criminals she'd help to put away. She'd done fairy tales and favorite books. This year, which would mark the ninth anniversary of the tradition she had started when she first moved into her own place at eighteen, she had decided her theme was a fairground, complete with moving carousel. She already had all the ingredients bought, and a plan drawn up and sitting on her kitchen counter waiting for tomorrow.

"I feel okay, I really do. Yes, sore, but nothing I can't handle," Chloe said as she pulled to a stop in front of a pretty white house with a beautiful garden.

"Okay." She'd let it go. If Chloe said she felt okay, then she had to believe that, even though it didn't look like she did. When she'd been recovering, she had hated the constant questions about how she was doing. She knew people only asked because they cared, but it had been annoying having to give the same answer over and over again.

"Careful when you get out, it's slippery," Chloe said as she climbed from the car.

Savannah was *always* careful. She couldn't afford another fall. If her bad hip was injured again, there was a chance she would lose the ability to walk. At first, her doctors had hoped to put in an artificial hip which would give her much better movement and less pain than she had now. But the damage to the entire area had been extensive, and they hadn't been able to guarantee that a replacement would work.

"I hope I'm able to help," she said as Chloe walked slowly with her up the garden path to the front door.

"Me too. Taylor is refusing to look at photos of Harley Zabkar to see if he's the man who abducted her. She says she doesn't want to know. Apparently, she has decided she just wants to forget about the whole thing and move on. But *we* need to know. The killer has Avery Ormont, so we need Taylor to tell us if Harley is her kidnapper or if it's Pete Larkin or someone else altogether."

"Fin can't ask her? I thought he had been helping her," she said slowly. She knew how much it had hurt her friend when she had walked away from the man she loved. Savannah really hoped they could work things out. If Fin would just admit to himself that his anger at Chloe was misplaced and he was really just feeling guilty, and if Chloe would just admit that what happened wasn't her fault and that she didn't deserve Fin's anger, then maybe they could.

"Apparently he made a clean break with her after yesterday," Chloe said as she rapped on the door.

"I can't believe she attacked you."

Chloe shrugged. "She's hurting and confused and traumatized and needed someone to lash out at. And that person just happens to be me. I think she thought of me as an obstacle in the way of her getting Fin, which is ridiculous given how adamant Fin has been about us never getting back together. But anyway, I don't know how receptive she's going to be to me, which is why you're here. I was hoping that maybe the fact that you'd nearly been abducted, and that you were able to ID the man who did it, and that you'd also suffered a broken bone at the hands of your attacker, that it might provide some common ground and you'll be able to get through to her."

Not that she minded helping, but she worked crime scene and collected evidence—she didn't interview victims and the prospect of doing it was a little unnerving. "Tom couldn't come?"

"Tom's working on trying to get Harley Zabkar's bail

revoked."

"I can't believe they gave him bail."

"Yeah, me neither," Chloe said quietly.

Knowing exactly where her friend's mind had just gone, Savannah said, "I can't believe Marcus King got out, either."

"It's crazy."

"Are you worried he's going to come after you?"

"No, not really. It's been a long time, and he knows I'm not a little kid anymore. But I am worried he's going to hurt more kids."

Despite her outward calm, Savannah could tell Chloe was worried. No victim wanted to know that the person who hurt them was free to come after them again or hurt someone else. She remembered the fear she'd felt when her would be abductor had still been on the loose. She'd had a police guard at the door of her hospital room every minute of the month it took to find and catch him.

Chloe rapped again on the door of Taylor's parents' house. Taylor was going to be staying with them while she recovered, and Savannah hoped it helped. It was nice to have the people who loved you around while you were healing; it made the long, painful process bearable.

Inside the house, something went bump.

"Did you hear that?" Chloe asked.

She nodded. "Do you think Taylor is okay? Maybe she fell."

"Maybe," Chloe agreed.

"Or maybe he came back for her."

The look on her friend's face said she was afraid of that. "Go wait in the car."

As if. "I'm not going anywhere. I know how to use a gun; otherwise, I wouldn't be able to do field work. Give me your backup, and I'll cover you."

It was clear Chloe wanted to argue, but they didn't have time for that, so she pulled out her backup and handed it over. Then she knocked on the door again. "Taylor, it's Agent Luckman, open up."

There was no response.

Chloe's hand went to the doorknob, which turned in her grip.

That was a bad sign.

Slowly, Chloe pushed the door open.

The house was dark and quiet, and the hairs on the back of her neck stood up.

Something felt wrong.

Although the sensible part of her brain told her to flee from potential trouble, her instincts were to help someone in need.

It was too quiet. If Taylor was here and able to, she would have let them know before now.

She hadn't.

That meant she either wasn't here or wasn't able to let them know.

The thump they had heard suggested that someone was in here.

They made their way through the foyer slowly and carefully, searching every nook, corner, and crevice for a potential threat.

Chloe was just moving to enter the first room on their right when she suddenly let out a yelp.

What happened next came so fast, Savannah didn't even have time to process it.

Someone launched at Chloe, knocking her to the ground, her weapon sliding uselessly out of reach.

Savannah dropped her cane, leaning back against the wall to keep her balance, but whoever had knocked down her friend had disappeared back into the dark house.

Something was wrong with Chloe. She was attempting to stand, but her movements were sluggish and awkward. Like she had lost the ability to use her limbs. She knew that uncoordinated look. Chloe had been drugged.

Keeping her gun trained on the doorway to the room where

their assailant was hiding, she pulled out her phone to call for help.

Only, she never made the call.

Someone shoved her violently from behind, and she lost her footing and fell.

The sudden sharp pain in her hip momentarily stole her ability to function.

Before she could reclaim it, something slammed into her bad hip, tossing her violently toward unconsciousness as pain exploded inside her, stealing her breath.

As she choked and wheezed and tried not to pass out, a voice spoke above her. "I'd take you with us, but you're already broken. I don't like broken things. Takes all the fun out of it. Your friend, on the other hand, she's coming with me."

The presence beside her left and Savannah forced herself to move.

She had to do something.

This man was going to take Chloe if she didn't.

She had dropped her weapon when she fell, and now she tried to blink the tears from her eyes enough to be able to see.

There it was.

Just a few feet away.

Somehow, she managed to roll to the gun, fighting to remain conscious as wave after wave of nauseating pain billowed her.

Her hands curled around the cool metal.

She lifted the weapon.

Tried to aim.

But the second blow to her hip caused her world to spiral into nothingness.

* * * * *

10:44 A.M.

Something felt wrong.

This probably wasn't the smartest thing he had ever done, but he was following Chloe. With Marcus King back on the streets, he was worried about her safety.

Fin was worried about her, period.

He had messed things up.

Big time.

He never should've taken his fear and guilt out on Chloe. He should never have allowed the anger he felt at the unfairness of losing his son out on the one person who was hurting as badly as he was.

But he was done with that.

He was done with being angry and feeling guilty.

He was going to do whatever it took to get Chloe to let him apologize to her, then he was going to do whatever it took to make things up to her.

It was time to stop living drenched in pain and anger. It was time to let it go and move on.

So, that's what he was trying to do, and the first thing he had to do was make sure that Chloe was safe.

He had followed her from her house to Savannah's, and then here. He wasn't quite sure where here was, but Chloe and Savannah had headed into a house across the street from where he was parked.

They had gone in about five minutes ago.

And now he had this feeling in his gut that said that Chloe wasn't okay.

It made no sense. Tom wasn't with her, so wherever she had gone, she hadn't thought it was dangerous.

Still, he couldn't shake the feeling.

Fin was debating whether he should go and check things out, which was going to make Chloe pretty mad if he was wrong and he interrupted whatever she was doing just because he had a panic attack.

Even if he was right, what was he going to do? He was a doctor, not an FBI agent or a cop. If Chloe were in trouble, how was he going to help her?

He was still debating when a single shot sliced through the air.

A gunshot.

Before he had time to process what he was doing, he was out of the car and running toward the house Chloe and Savannah had entered.

That the gunshot had come from a different house never even occurred to him.

He didn't stop running until he stepped through the door.

Both Chloe and Savannah lay in crumpled heaps on the floor.

He didn't see blood.

Who had been shot?

Fin started toward Chloe when something sharp pricked his leg.

He batted at it, found a syringe embedded in his calf.

Someone had drugged him.

His limbs began to tingle, and his vision blurred. Any minute he was going to pass out and then what would happen to them? What would happen to Chloe? Was she even still alive?

She was so still.

She hadn't roused as he'd entered the house.

He tried to go to her, but his legs began to tremble then gave out, and he landed hard on his knees. He shuffled toward her as best as he could as his limbs grew heavier and more uncooperative.

He had to get to her.

He had to know that she was still alive.

He would fight with every fiber of his being if she was.

"Chloe." He tried to say her name, but his voice box was seizing up, and it came out rough and gravelly.

She was so close and yet so far away.

Finally, he reached her, pressed his fingertips to her throat. He thought he felt a pulse, but his fingers were mostly numb.

Fin slumped to the floor beside her, trying to drag her to him so he could protect her as best he could.

Which was pretty much not at all.

How could he protect her when his spinning head was about to throw him off the merry-go-round and into oblivion?

He had messed up.

He should have called for help before coming in here.

And now it was too late.

Blackness came down and covered him.

Fin didn't know how much time had passed when he first started to climb his way back to consciousness.

It took a moment for everything to come rushing back.

The gunshot.

Finding Chloe and Savannah unconscious.

Being drugged.

His eyes snapped open, and he would have bolted upright, but his limbs were still heavy.

Fear laced his blood, traveling around every inch of his body.

Chloe was no longer in his arms.

Wildly, he searched the room, but she wasn't there.

She was gone.

But Savannah wasn't. She still lay right where she'd been when he'd stupidly come running in here.

What he should have done was call Tom, then sit and watch the house until he got there.

Pity he was smart about it now and not when it had mattered.

Staggering to his feet, he hurried to Savannah and dropped down at her side. Had she been drugged, too? If she had, she should have woken up by now—she'd been drugged first, so she should already be coming around. Unless he'd given her too much. He doubted whoever had attacked them had measured out the appropriate doses proportionate to their respective sizes.

Fin spotted blood on her hip.

Maybe she hadn't been drugged.

He checked for a pulse and found one, although it was weak and erratic.

Carefully, he probed her injury. As he eased down the waist of her skirt, so he could see it, he winced.

Savannah's hip was a mangled mess.

It looked like someone had kicked her hard enough to shatter her already injured hip. With how it looked, she would be lucky if she'd ever be able to walk again.

Panic was making it hard for him to concentrate. He wanted to find Chloe. The man who'd knocked him out had taken her. Given that Savannah had a broken—most likely shattered—bone, he was terrified it was The Breaker. She had obviously gone looking for him, only he had been prepared and gotten her first. But why leave Savannah behind? And him?

As much as he'd love to go running off and search for Chloe, pointless may it be, Savannah needed him.

He had to splint her leg.

The drugs had mostly left his system now, and he jumped to his feet, running through the house in search of anything he could use. He returned a couple of minutes later with a blanket and a sheet that he ripped into strips. Rolling up the blanket, he put it between her legs, then used the strips to secure her bad leg to her good one.

She was pale, and when he pressed the back of his hand to her cheek, her skin was clammy.

Savannah was going into shock.

Fin pulled out his phone and was about to call for help when she stirred and tried to move.

Fighting his fears, he tried to keep himself composed. If he panicked, she would panic, and right now, he needed to keep her calm.

"Hey, Savannah, it's Fin. Can you hear me?"

"Fin?" she murmured, her eyelashes fluttering on her cheeks as she tried to open her eyes.

"Try to stay still," he said, his hands on her shoulders to stop her from moving as she continued to squirm.

"My leg," she whimpered. Her eyes finally managed to open and looked up at him, filled with fear.

"It's all right. You'll be okay," he soothed, hoping it was true.

From the look in her eyes, she knew he was lying. "Where's Chloe?" she asked as she tried to search the room.

"Stay still," he said, sharper than he'd intended, but he was struggling to hold it together.

"She's gone. He took her and Taylor," Savannah said, her eyes falling closed.

Taylor? This must be Taylor's parents' house. Chloe and Savannah must have come here to talk to her. Only instead, they must have stumbled on the killer coming back to reclaim Taylor.

Now he had her back.

And he had Chloe, too.

"Savannah, did you see him?" If she had seen him, then at least they would know who they were looking for.

She didn't answer.

She'd passed out again.

She was shaking, and he spread out the other blanket he'd brought with him over her. It should help to keep her warm until help arrived.

Finding his phone where he'd dropped it on the floor beside him, he dialed Tom.

"Fin? Is something wrong?" Tom asked when he answered.

"I was following Chloe."

"What? Why? Because of Marcus King?"

"I didn't want him to come after her. She went to Taylor's parents' house."

"I know. She took Savannah to see if they could get Taylor to look at photos of Harley and Pete to tell us if either one of them is the killer."

"I know."

"How?" Tom sounded concerned now.

"There was a gunshot. I went inside. Someone drugged me. I just woke up, I don't know how long I was out. But Savannah is hurt. Badly. She needs an ambulance. And Chloe ..." He trailed off, unable to say the words out loud because it seemed to make them so much more real. "Chloe is gone."

* * * * *

2:36 P.M.

She had no idea where she was.

Chloe sensed multiple people in the room, so she tried her best to keep as still as she could while she tried to process exactly what was going on.

She remembered talking to Savannah as they drove to Taylor Sallow's parents' house to talk to her about looking at photos to ID her abductor.

She remembered hearing a clunk inside.

She remembered she and Savannah going in.

She remembered a sharp prick in her leg and then intense dizziness.

She remembered losing control of her body.

Then nothing.

Someone had drugged her. She could still feel the effect of the drugs lingering in her system.

It didn't take a genius to figure out she had been kidnapped.

Had Savannah been taken, too? And what about Taylor?

Carefully, she cracked her eyes open, trying to search the room without alerting whoever might be about that she was awake. If it were possible, she wanted to try to keep the element of surprise on her side.

As soon as she saw the room she was in, Chloe knew where

she was.

She'd known as soon as she felt the jab of the syringe in her leg, but now she couldn't deny it.

The Breaker had come back for Taylor, and she and Savannah had stumbled upon the kidnapping. He had obviously decided to take them with him.

Savannah.

She had to know if her friend was okay.

Chloe opened her eyes the rest of the way and saw Taylor sitting in a chair at a table. No, not just sitting in it—*tied* to it. Handcuffs circled her wrists, securing them to the arms of the chair. Avery Ormont was lying on a bed in the corner. She wasn't tied up, but then again there didn't seem to be much need to restrain her; there was a bulky cast on one leg, and one of her hands was heavily bandaged.

She had to find a way out of here.

If she didn't, she was going to wind up like Avery, with too many broken bones to be able to put up a fight.

And she would fight this man with everything she had.

Chloe went to sit up and was surprised when she was jerked back and pain shot through her shoulders.

Her arms were extended out at the sides and secured at the wrists and elbows with leather straps to an examining table of sorts. Her legs were also secured, at the ankles and knees. She wasn't going anywhere.

How had she not noticed that she was tied up?

Her jerky movements drew the attention of Taylor. "You're finally awake," the younger woman stated.

"How long?" she asked. Or tried to. Her throat was dry and sandpapery, and it hurt to talk.

"At least an hour or two," came Taylor's somewhat sullen reply. Chloe knew that Taylor didn't like her, but she was going to have to get over it. If they were going to get out of here alive, then they were going to need to work together.

He'd probably given her too much of whatever sedative he used since he hadn't been expecting her to turn up. He had brought her and Taylor to wherever he was keeping Avery, so why hadn't he brought Savannah?

Had he killed her?

Pain and fear filled her. She couldn't let herself think that her best friend might be dead. She had to keep her wits about her. Savannah wasn't here, and that had to be a good thing. Maybe he just hadn't been able to juggle three unconscious women, so he'd left her behind. Maybe Savannah would be able to ID the killer when she woke up, assuming the man had drugged her, as well.

Since she was restrained, the most valuable thing she could get at the moment was information. She had to gather as much of it as she could.

"What happened, Taylor?"

Tears brimmed in her green eyes. She was close to falling apart. "I needed some space. Time on my own to think. I asked my parents if they could leave me alone for a bit, so they did. He must have been waiting for me to be alone because they'd only been gone ten minutes or so when he came. I was making hot chocolate. I always loved to drink it at Christmas when I was a kid. I thought it might help. I was looking for marshmallows when I felt a prick on my back. I didn't hear him." She began to cry softly.

"Do you remember anything else after that?"

Taylor shook her head. "I remember getting dizzy, and my body started to tingle and go numb, and then I must have passed out. Just like the day he took me the first time. I woke up when he was putting the handcuffs on."

Frustrated, Chloe struggled restlessly against her bonds. Taylor didn't know anything helpful. She turned her attention to the other woman. "Hi, Avery."

"You know me?" came the part-confused, part-relieved reply.

"My name is Chloe Luckman, I'm an FBI agent. My partner

and I were looking for you. We had a couple of suspects; we were going to talk to Taylor and try to find out who it was when he grabbed us."

"So, you don't know who he is?" Avery awkwardly propped herself up on her elbows as best she could.

"No. Sorry. But my partner will figure it out. There was a friend of mine with me when I went to Taylor's house—a colleague—he didn't bring her with us so she might be able to identify him."

"Or she's already dead," Taylor said dejectedly.

Chloe grabbed hold of the fear before it could get a foothold inside her. She couldn't let herself think that Savannah was already dead. "Do you know anything about him, Avery, that might help us?"

"Not really. He calls himself The Breaker. He wants to try to break all my bones one at a time before he kills me. He's done it before." She inclined her head at one of the walls where there were four large skeleton pictures hung on the wall. There were black marks on various parts of the pictures. "One is mine and the others are his other victims."

"The third one is me," Taylor said quietly.

"*You're* one of his victims?" Avery sounded shocked. "He didn't tell me one of his victims was still alive. I thought they were all dead."

"You did as he wanted," Taylor said. "You have a cast on and a morphine drip. You must have done what he wanted."

"What?" Chloe asked, confused.

"He doesn't really care about inflicting pain. If you do as he says, he gives you a local anesthetic before he breaks a bone. Morphine, too. I didn't the first time, and he broke my thumb and refused to set it. I didn't want to do it." Avery's pale cheeks tinted pink. "But I didn't know what else to do. I didn't think I could survive the next break without the painkillers. I was lucky the first time, I only got a three. I wouldn't have survived this two if I hadn't told him I'd do whatever he wanted."

"You got a three? A two? What does that mean?" she asked.

"You don't want to know," Taylor said.

Avery nodded, then lay back down against her pillows. "He said something about doing the breaks closer together. He thinks it will give my body less of a chance to shut down. He's going to break one every forty-eight hours until he's done or until I die, whatever comes first." The last she said dully like she was already resigned to her fate.

Avery may be resigned to being tortured and dying here in this room—Taylor, too—but she certainly wasn't. There was a way to escape. Taylor had done it once already. Now there were three of them. They could do this.

"Taylor, how did you escape last time?"

"What does it matter? This time he has us all tied up. Last time I was free to move about the room."

"There are three of us now. We can do it, Taylor. We can. Don't give up hope yet. What did you do to get away from him last time?"

Taylor sighed but answered anyway. "He was ready to break another one of my bones after my leg. I don't remember doing it, but he went to put the local anesthetic in my leg, and I just grabbed it. I caught him by surprise. I'd been so obedient up until then. I shoved it into his leg and pushed the plunger. He fell, and I just jumped up and ran. I think he must have left the key in the door, I don't remember, I just remember stabbing him with the needle and running."

Anesthetic.

That was a good idea.

The girls said that if they played along, pretended to be obedient, did as he asked, then he would reward them by making sure they weren't in pain.

She could take advantage of that.

She could play the game, do as he asked, then when he came at her, she could get him with the anesthetic, and they could escape.

That they were tied up presented a problem, but not an insurmountable one. If she or Taylor or both of them could get free, then they stood an even better chance of getting away. She couldn't get out of the leather straps on her own, but if Avery or Taylor could get to her, they could untie her. That way, when he came to break one of her bones, she could get him with the syringe, then they could run. If they couldn't run, then stabbing him with the syringe wasn't going to do them any good.

So, how to get untied?

* * * * *

11:50 P.M.

"Is she awake?"

Fin looked up as Tom entered Savannah's hospital room. He'd been sitting in here, keeping vigil, as though by staying close to Savannah he was holding on to something that linked him to Chloe, and thus felt closer to her.

Tiredly, he scrubbed his hands over his face. It had been over twelve hours since Chloe went missing and they had been the longest twelve hours of his life.

He wanted to go looking for her, but where would he start?

Tom and Chloe hadn't even been sure who the killer was, let alone where he was hiding his victims.

But just sitting here was hell.

He felt so useless. So impotent. Just like he had the night his son had died.

Now, with Chloe missing, possibly dead, the anger he'd harbored toward her all seemed so stupid. So meaningless. While he had been nursing his rage, sulking because Chloe had just been another person to walk out on him, he'd missed out on so much time with her. They could have helped each other grieve; they could have helped each other heal.

Instead, they had both been lost and alone.

She had walked away, and he hadn't done a thing to stop her.

He had been selfish and stupid.

There were so many things he might have done. So many things he *should* have done. But anger was easy. It was comfortable. He'd been angry at his parents, his grandparents, and even his sister. They'd all abandoned him. He had never thought that Chloe would do it, too.

Pain and tragedy were supposed to bring you closer together. The loss of their son should have cemented their love. Instead, they had both tossed it away as they struggled with their guilt and the responsibility they each felt for the death of their son.

Chloe was wrong to bail, but he was just as wrong to let her.

He should have stopped it from happening. Instead of letting guilt and anger consume him, he should have grabbed hold of the woman he loved and told her he loved her, and that he was so sorry their son was gone. He should have held her, kissed her, made love to her, talked to her—he should have just loved her.

Should haves.

Would haves.

Could haves.

None of them did him any good.

He'd done what he had, and although now he wanted nothing more than to hold Chloe and tell her how sorry he was, he couldn't.

He had made mistakes.

Big ones.

And now it might be too late to rectify them.

Chloe might already be dead. And if she wasn't, if they found her in time, Fin knew he wouldn't get her back in one piece.

If his prayers were answered and Chloe was rescued, he knew he would be sitting beside her hospital bed just as he was sitting beside Savannah's.

"She's in and out," he finally replied. "When she's awake, she's pretty out of it; they have her pumped up on a lot of drugs."

"She's stable, though?"

"Yes."

"And her leg? How did her surgery go?"

"It went as well as can be expected, considering the extent of the damage," he replied vaguely.

"What does that mean? Will she be able to walk?"

"There's no way to know yet. We'll have to wait to see when she's stronger and she can get up and to physical therapy."

"Fin." Tom looked exasperated.

He looked up to meet his eye. "There's a chance she'll be able to walk again with a lot of hard work and therapy. But there's a good chance the damage is too extreme. I'm not an orthopedic surgeon, but from what I saw of her injury, and from talking to her doctor, I'd say there's about a thirty percent chance she'll walk."

"Does she know yet?" Tom asked grimly.

"No. Her brother wanted to wait until she was stronger before she's told, and she hasn't been awake long enough to really talk to her."

"Do you think she'll wake up soon? I need to know what she saw."

Tom had been trying to talk to Savannah ever since he'd arrived at Taylor's parents' house, shortly after the local cops and EMTs. But even when she was awake, she had been in too much pain to be able to say much of anything. Then the medics had dosed her up with morphine and sedatives and rushed her to the hospital. In the emergency room, she had continued to hover in and out but wasn't lucid enough to give a statement.

Fin knew that it wasn't Tom being cold. He cared about Savannah. They all did. But she was the only one who had seen the killer. At least, they hoped she had. She was the one who had fired the shot that he'd heard, so the chances were that she had seen whoever attacked her and kidnapped Chloe and Taylor before he hurt her.

"Did you see *any*thing?" Tom asked.

Although he'd already answered the agent's questions, he complied again. Anything to help Chloe. And who knew, maybe he would remember something else the more times he told his story. "When I went in, all I saw was Chloe and Savannah on the floor. Neither of them was moving. I knew something was wrong. I went to check on them, and something sharp pricked me. I got dizzy and numb. I managed to get to Chloe before I passed out, but I didn't see anyone else. When I woke up, it was just me and Savannah."

"Did you see a car parked out front? In the driveway?"

"I wasn't paying attention. I didn't even know whose house it was. I was just there to follow Chloe and keep an eye on her. As far as I remember, there were no cars in the driveway."

"Did you hear anything?"

Fin thought about that. "Footsteps maybe just before I passed out."

"Did you smell anything?"

His brow furrowed as he thought. Something came back to him. "A musty smell. Like mothballs, maybe." He wished he could give Tom more than that. He wished a lot of things. Most notably, he wished he had done things differently this morning. "I'm sorry, Tom. I shouldn't have gone in. I should have called. I wasn't thinking. If I had called and watched the house until help arrived, then Chloe and Taylor would still be here, and you'd have your man."

"You couldn't have known what was going on in there," Tom consoled him.

Savannah moaned, and Fin immediately snapped his attention to her. Levering himself out of his chair, he went to the bed and picked up her wrist to check her pulse. "Savannah? You with me?"

Her eyes opened almost impossibly slowly, as though it was an enormous feat for her to lift her lids.

Although he wanted to rip out whatever answers she had in her head, Fin forced himself to be gentle with her. Savannah might be the only one who could tell them what they needed to get Chloe back. "How's your pain?"

"Okay," her voice was slurred, and her pupils were dilated. The medications dripping from the IV into the back of her hand had her so spaced out, he wasn't sure she'd be able to tell them anything.

"Do you think you can answer a couple of questions?"

She nodded. "Chloe?"

"What do you remember?" Tom asked, standing on the other side of her bed.

"We heard something ... went inside ... Chloe cried out ... fell ... pain in my hip ..." She haltingly related the story.

As she mentioned her hip, her eyes cleared.

Fin knew she was going to ask about it even before she opened her mouth.

"How bad is it?"

"Don't worry about that now," Tom soothed, trying to distract her.

Apparently, she was with it enough not to be fooled. Her blue eyes were watery, and she was trembling. "That bad."

"When you're strong enough, you'll do physical therapy. It'll get better. Really, you shouldn't be worrying about that now. Right now, you just rest and to get your strength back," he tried to reassure her. There would be time for her to worry about whether or not she'd walk again when she wasn't so emotional and vulnerable.

"Savannah," Tom drew her attention back to him. "The man who attacked you, did you get a look at him?"

She shook her head. They were going to lose her at any minute, whatever reserves of strength she had built up while she'd been sleeping were now used up.

Tom looked disappointed but patted her hand. "Sleep now, and we'll talk to you again later."

Savannah's eyes closed, and Fin thought she had passed out again. But then she spoke, "He said something to me. He said I was broken and he didn't like broken things. His voice. I recognized it. I know who he is. He was my physical therapist for a while. His name is Pete Larkin."

DECEMBER 24TH

12:13 A.M.

Three women at once. Was he crazy?

He had to be, Pete thought to himself.

What had he been thinking? He should have just left the FBI agent behind with her partner. She had bruises, after all, so she wasn't completely perfect.

Bruises, but no broken bones.

That was the important thing. He had checked after she passed out, probed the areas around the bruising to make sure she was still in good condition. It was too bad about the other FBI agent. She was beautiful, but he knew her, she was already broken, and it was so much more fun to break perfect things.

The agent—according to her badge, her name was Chloe Luckman—was pretty, too, although a little older than he typically liked. Still, it would certainly be fun to spend some time with her. She had to be tough and strong—if there was anyone whose body could survive what he was trying to accomplish, then it was certainly hers.

Pete was so excited. He had been on a high ever since he saw Taylor Sallow's parents drive away without her. He'd been worried the cops might keep someone on her, but because he had already taken Avery Ormont, they must have thought that he wasn't going to go back for her.

Well, they were wrong.

He always finished what he started.

And now, not only did he get to finish what he started with Taylor, but he had two other women to play with. That meant he could try out different methods with each of them to see what worked best. While he was hopeful that one of the three would be the one, he couldn't count on it, and every piece of information he learned would help him get closer to achieving his goals.

He was thinking he might stick with the original plan with Taylor, waiting until each bone was mostly healed before breaking another. Then with the FBI agent, he thought he would break one a day and see if breaking the bones quicker and closer together was a better idea. Then with Avery, he might give her just a few days in between breaks—maybe a week, but no more—and see if some sort of middle ground was, in fact, the best method.

He was too excited.

He couldn't wait.

Although it was the middle of the night, he wasn't sleeping, and he didn't think the girls would be either. It had been a big day for them, and for him, and he wanted to finish it off with some fun.

Sleep was overrated. Who cares if he was a wreck at work tomorrow—it wasn't like anyone was going to guess he had stayed up all night playing with his girls. Well, *working* with them. This wasn't really a game; it was the culmination of his life's work. It was his dream.

Tossing on some clothes, he headed for the secret room.

Even if by some weird coincidence the FBI managed to latch on to him as a suspect, and he couldn't really see that happening, they had no reason to even be thinking about him. But in case they did, they could search this house from top to bottom and still never find the room.

As he unlocked the door, he did his best to contain his glee. Yes, he was excited, but if he got overexcited, then there was a possibility that he could make a mistake. A *small* possibility, but there was still a chance it could happen.

It had happened before.

With Taylor.

He hadn't thought the girl had it in her to try to escape.

Still, that had taught him a valuable lesson, and he would never be that careless again.

The chances of that scenario repeating itself were slim. Since he now had three girls, he had to do things a little differently. And that meant making sure that they were secured. No longer could he let them wander around the room. Especially in this early stage while they were uninjured. Maybe once the FBI agent had a few broken bones, he might rethink that, but for now, each girl would remain restrained.

"Wakey, wakey, girlie girls," he sang as he opened the door.

Three sets of eyes—scared eyes—turned to look at him.

"Pete Larkin." Chloe looked at him in thinly-veiled surprise.

She knew him?

How?

He was sure he didn't know her.

Wait, maybe she was friends with the other agent who had been with her at the house? That could make sense because he remembered that other agent from a few years ago. She had been a patient at the rehab facility where he worked, so if they were friends, then it was possible that Chloe had met him then.

But if that were true, then why would she remember him?

He tried not to make too much of an impression on any of the people he met there—he wanted to be able to study the various injuries without anyone noticing. He spent hours poring over x-rays and doctor's reports, learning everything he could.

His gaze narrowed as he zeroed in on her. "How do you know me?"

"Your reputation of being overly interested in patients with broken bones put you on our radar, but ..." She trailed off, seemingly rethinking divulging whatever information she had been about to let loose.

So, the FBI was on to him.

That certainly changed things.

He should have killed the other agent. He hadn't because he didn't want to. He didn't like killing broken things. It was so much more fun to break perfect things. But that had been a mistake; there was a chance she might be able to identify him. If she remembered him from the facility, then she could tell them who he was.

Maybe he shouldn't do this tonight.

If he had to pack up and move, then having to take three injured girls with him would complicate things. He had other properties he could go to, but he'd have to wait until they were fitted out with a special room. In the meantime, he didn't really have another choice but to remain here and hope for the best.

So, if he had to remain here anyway, he may as well have some fun first.

"You were in an accident when you were just a baby, only two years old," Chloe was saying. "Is that when you got interested in broken bones?"

"I don't remember the accident. I was too young," he answered honestly. Although, despite the fact he didn't remember that time in his life, he assumed it was safe to say that yes, that was when his obsession had begun.

"You were in the hospital for over a year. That's a long time for anyone—especially such a little boy," she continued.

Pete knew what she was trying to do. She was trying to gather information that she could use against him.

But what could she do with anything he told her?

She was strapped to an examination table inside his secret room. She wasn't going anywhere.

He may as well indulge her a little. "It was. It was also the only time my parents were actually around. They traveled a lot for work. Left me with nannies. But after the accident, they stayed with me while I was in the hospital recovering. Once I was better, they were gone again."

"You started breaking things after that." The look in her eyes now held a small touch of sympathy.

"Toys at first, then windows and valuables they had laying around the house."

"That didn't work, though."

"They were afraid to punish me because I'd nearly died. I *should* have died. The doctors don't know how I survived. I had over one hundred broken bones. But somehow, I survived. I liked breaking things. It gave me a sense of control—of peace, even. I started breaking animal bones next. I'd set traps for squirrels and birds and snap each one of their little bones. They always died, though," he said, perplexed. He had survived and yet, others didn't. He had only made it into the nineties with Christie, and she had been his biggest success so far, yet he still hadn't gotten even close to finishing.

"You were trying to figure out why you lived and they didn't," Chloe said quietly.

"I started breaking my own bones next. I wanted to see what was different about me."

"Did that bring your parents' home?"

"No. They just sent me more stuff. But I didn't want *stuff*," he said disgustedly. He didn't care about toys and clothes and video games and cars. They didn't interest him. He only had one interest, one hobby, one obsession. Breaking things.

"You wanted to try to kill someone by breaking every single bone in their body."

He looked at Chloe, confused. "I don't want to kill them. I want to prove that it's possible to break every bone in someone's body and have them survive. And you are going to help me do it."

* * * * *

12:48 A.M.

What?

Pete Larkin didn't want to kill anyone?

He was just delusional enough to believe that he could pull off breaking every bone in someone's body and yet keep them alive.

Which was exactly what he was going to try to do to her, Taylor, and Avery if their plan didn't work.

Chloe prayed that it would.

Avery was anxiously watching Pete Larkin's every move. The teenager had been able to untie her. She'd had to drag herself across the floor to do it. Apparently, Pete brought her crutches to use to get to and from the toilet, but he took them with him when he left. He wanted to make sure that Avery was stuck on the bed.

But he had underestimated Avery.

The girl had gritted her teeth, swung her broken leg off the bed, lowered herself to the floor, and used her arms to pull herself along, all the while whimpering and holding back her screams. Somehow, Avery had managed to pull herself to her feet—well, foot—and untied one of Chloe's arms.

Chloe had wanted to be completely free; she hated the feeling of being confined and helpless. But she hadn't known who her abductor was. He could have come in here armed, and with Taylor still cuffed to the chair, and Avery with one leg in a cast, she wasn't sure she'd be able to take him. She was well trained, but the man who had kidnapped them was no doubt going to be big. There was nothing she could see in here that would work as a weapon, and she couldn't risk the others being hurt if she couldn't overpower him.

So, she'd just had Avery loosen one of her wrists. She didn't want Pete to know that she was free. She wanted to catch him unawares. And right now, it looked like she was safely restrained, just as Pete had left her.

To cross the room, Avery had had to rip out her IV, and she was paranoid that Pete was going to notice and their whole plan would be blown before they even got a chance to execute it.

Chloe silently willed the girl to remain calm. They didn't want to give Pete any reason to suspect anything.

Pete set down the box of supplies he had brought in with him by the examining table she was on and barely spared her a glance. Instead, he headed to Taylor, running a hand almost lovingly through her hair.

"I'm glad to have you back," he said. "Your leg looks like its healing nicely. You'll be ready for your next one soon."

"No, please," Taylor whimpered, attempting to shrink away from him.

The slap echoed in the small room.

Taylor shrieked and began to cry.

"I see we need to work on your manners. You've regressed while you've been gone." Pete sounded annoyed.

Although he claimed he wasn't really interested in killing anyone, he had also freely admitted that he enjoyed breaking things. She and the others were merely objects in his mind. Objects he intended to shatter. If this didn't work and they couldn't get free, then the best she could do was play along, soak up whatever mercies in the form of painkillers and anesthetics he was willing to offer, and pray that her partner was able to find her before she was too broken to put back together.

"How's *your* leg feeling, Avery?" He headed to the bed.

Even from here, Chloe could see Avery was shaking.

"It-it's fine," Avery stuttered.

Any hope he wouldn't notice the ripped out IV was quickly squashed. "What happened to your IV?"

"I'm sorry," Avery said quickly, and Chloe was sure she was going to spill everything, but then she said, "I was sleeping. It came out. I must have been tossing and turning. I didn't mean to."

Chloe held her breath, waiting for Pete's response. She had the feeling Taylor and Avery were doing the same thing.

"You don't have to be sorry for that, Avery." Pete picked up her arm. "I'll just put it back in." He cleaned the small cut on the inside of her elbow where she'd pulled out the needle, then started a new IV in the back of her hand.

They were in the clear.

So far, he had bought everything.

But the hard part was coming up.

Chloe prayed she could keep herself under control and pretend she was still tied up when he came to her. She had a feeling he hadn't just come in here to check in with them.

He was here to hurt them.

More specifically, hurt *her*.

Since she was the only one whom he hadn't injured yet, she knew she was next. And by the looks of him, he was anxious to get to it.

She hoped she could do this.

She hoped it worked.

But she was having major doubts.

She'd been wrong before. She had been so sure that the killer was Harley Zabkar, but it wasn't. Her gut had been wrong. Maybe he really had been so desperate for money that he'd gone to a loan shark, and when he'd been unable to pay it back, they'd threatened him. Maybe he really hadn't heard them identify themselves as FBI agents and had shot at them because he thought they were there to hurt him.

If she'd been wrong about that, then maybe she was wrong about her plan.

Her gut obviously wasn't something she could trust yet.

She had messed up by going to Taylor's house with just Savannah. She never should have taken her friend, who could be dead because of her. She should have known that the killer would never have let Taylor go even if he had found a new victim. She should have anticipated this. She should have made sure that they put someone on Taylor. She should have been more careful when they walked into the house. She should have noticed him hiding in the room. She shouldn't have let him drug her.

So many should haves.

Tom had always told her that she couldn't be impulsive. That she had to be more careful. She hadn't listened to him. She'd thought that as long as catching the bad guys was her number one priority, then everything else would be okay.

Now, everything was messed up, Savannah might be dead, and soon she could be, too.

If she made it out of this, she would never be this careless again. She was going to make sure that she paid attention to everything. *Every*thing.

That wasn't the only thing she was going to change.

She was going to make things work with Fin.

She didn't care if he said he didn't want to get back together. He was lying to her and to himself. He still loved her; he was just afraid that if he let go of that anger, then he would have to feel the full force of the grief that the death of their son caused.

Chloe knew because she had been doing the same thing.

But no more.

They were going to sit down and talk and make things right.

They loved each other, and in the end, that was what mattered.

To do that, she needed to get out of here.

"You're very pretty." Pete appeared at her side, tracing his fingertips down her cheek. She shivered, and not in the good kind of way like she did when Fin's fingers touched her body, but in the bad kind of helpless in the hands of a psychotic serial killer kind of way. "I like pretty things."

Did he want a response of some sort?

She wasn't sure what to say to him that wasn't going to upset him. She knew he wanted complete and utter obedience. She was here to serve one purpose, and that was to stay alive while he broke her bones. So long as she did that, he was pleased with her. Anything else was just going to annoy him.

So, she said nothing.

"Ah, you're a good girl." He nodded approvingly. "And you

might be the one to actually help me do this. Your body is perfect."

Chloe couldn't stop the repulsed shudder as he ran his hands up and down her body, squeezing her arms and legs. At least she knew he didn't sexually assault his victims. That was one positive thing she had going for her.

At least, she thought he didn't.

His hand came to a stop on her breast, and he squeezed it, his eyes glazing over. He found her attractive. She was a little older than his other victims, a little closer in age to him.

"So soft," he murmured under his breath.

The hand on her breast began to knead, and it took every bit of self-control she had not to lash out at him with the one hand she had free. She would have, only that would have ruined everything. He hadn't gotten the drugs out yet. If she tipped him off now, then she'd never have a chance to escape.

He dipped his head, slowly, as though he weren't really aware of what he was doing. His lips touched hers ever so softly, and then he seemed to snap back to reality. He straightened and pinched her cheek like one might do to a baby. "Maybe later." He gave her what she figured he thought was a beguiling smile. "But that's not what you're here for. I'll roll the dice."

The dice?

Was this what the girls meant when they were talking about numbers earlier?

Pete picked up a large foam dice and tossed it up in the air. It landed a couple of feet away and rolled over a few times before coming to a stop on the other side of the room.

"You got a four," he announced cheerfully when he'd retrieved it.

A four? Was that good or bad?

"Fours are arms," he explained as he came back over. "But don't worry, since you've been good and haven't caused me any trouble, you get the drugs. Taylor," he paused and looked over his shoulder, "since you were a little bratty earlier, next time, you don't."

Chloe tried her best to regulate her breathing. She couldn't hyperventilate; she needed to hold it together. There was no need to be afraid; she was going to stop him before he hurt her.

He pulled a small vial from the box he'd brought with him earlier. "This is the local anesthetic. I'll inject it near your shoulder, wait a minute or two, and then with my hammer," he paused and picked up a hammer, "I'll break the bone. Then I'll set up an IV with morphine, and fluids to keep you hydrated."

Pete made it sound so simple. Like abducting someone, tying them up, and breaking their bones was the most normal thing in the world.

She kept her focus on the syringe, and not on what Pete was saying. If she focused on him, she was going to lose it, and she was only getting one chance at this.

All she had to do was wait until he was moving the syringe toward her shoulder, then grab his arm and push it toward him. She had to make sure her aim was spot on, she needed to get him in the leg like Taylor had. Then he'd lose his balance, fall, and give her enough time to get her other hand and legs free.

Once she was free, she'd find something to use to tie him up, or she'd give him more local anesthetic so he couldn't stand at all, or she'd use the hammer if she had to and knock him unconscious.

If Taylor had done it, then she could do it.

His hand came toward her.

At the last second, she made her move.

Her free hand swung up and wrapped around Pete's wrist. Caught off guard, she was able to shove it in the direction of his leg and was rewarded by a sharp gasp as the needle pierced his skin. She depressed the plunger, and the drug filled his system.

Pete wobbled, his face contorted into a mask of pure rage.

As he fell, the hammer came up and then down.

Landing with a sickening thud on her arm.

Chloe felt the snap.

White hot pain ripped through her body.

She tried not to scream.

She bit her teeth into her lip so hard she tasted blood.

Her stomach roiled.

Bile bubbled up.

She turned her head to the side and vomited.

Even that small movement was enough to toss her headlong toward unconsciousness. She would have blacked out, only she heard a voice.

Tom's voice.

She was saved.

* * * * *

1:22 A.M.

"You should wait in the car."

Fin just looked at Tom like he'd lost his mind.

"Backup should be here any minute, you should wait here for them."

"I'm not staying out here, and I'm not waiting another minute. Chloe is in there." He needed to get to her. Now. The longer she was in the hands of that maniac, the greater the chances that she'd be hurt.

"Fin—"

"Whatever you're going to say, don't bother. I'm going in there right now with or without you."

He didn't bother waiting to hear Tom's response, just flung open the car door and started for Pete Larkin's house. He wished he had a gun on him, but that wasn't going to stop him.

He was at the front door when Tom caught up to him. "We should wait."

"Then wait."

"Fin," Tom sounded exasperated.

"If it were Hannah in there, would you sit around out here and wait?"

Tom sighed. "No. Which is the only reason I didn't handcuff you to the steering wheel. You can shoot, right?"

"Right." He wasn't great, but he and Chloe had gone to the shooting range a few times, and she'd taught him well. He could handle a weapon and hit his target. Not a bullseye, but pretty close.

"Here." Tom handed over his backup weapon. "At least stay behind me."

He nodded, although he didn't promise that.

All he cared about was getting Chloe out of this house, and he would do whatever was necessary to do it.

They opened the door and stepped inside. The house was quiet. It was after midnight, so Pete Larkin was probably in bed asleep.

At least, that's what Fin kept telling himself.

Because the alternative was that he was with Chloe.

Hurting her.

Breaking her bones.

"Behind me," Tom hissed when he headed for the stairs. "We have to clear down here first."

Fighting the urge to ignore the FBI agent and go running wildly through the house in search of Chloe, he trailed behind Tom as they cleared the ground floor. If he hadn't been concerned about endangering Chloe further, then he would have thrown caution to the wind.

As it was, he clutched the gun in a death grip and helped to check each room, expecting a monster to come jumping out at any second.

Once they had cleared the first floor, they headed to the second.

Now that they were so close to Chloe, time seemed to have slowed. Each step felt like he was dragging his feet through quicksand.

They cleared the second floor and headed to the third.

So far, they hadn't found Pete's bedroom. It had to be up here. The man clearly lived here. There had been dirty clothes in the laundry room, the fridge had been stocked, and there were dirty dishes in the sink.

There had also been no sign of Chloe and the others.

They had to be around here somewhere.

At least, he hoped so.

But Pete Larkin was wealthy. Unbelievably wealthy. His family owned a number of properties, and just because he lived here, didn't mean that he kept his victims here.

If Chloe wasn't here, then he would *make* the man tell him where she was.

The way he was feeling right now, he would do anything necessary to make it happen. Whatever it took. He'd threaten him, he'd lie to him, he'd hurt him if need be.

Anything.

Even if that meant beating it out of the man. He would gladly go to prison if it meant Chloe was safe and sound.

He froze as they entered the last bedroom on this floor.

Mothballs.

"Tom," he whispered.

"Yeah, I smell it."

They were close. Chloe was here. Somewhere. "Covers are mussed."

"Bathroom." Tom nodded at the closed door on the other side of the room, but Fin's gaze fell on the open door of the walk-in closet.

Mothballs.

People kept clothes in mothballs.

She was in the closet, he knew it.

Grabbing hold of Tom as he started for the bathroom, he gestured at the closet. Tom's eyes widened in understanding, and they both headed for the wardrobe.

Inside the closet looked normal, but at the end was a door. It looked like a safe room. The kind rich people sometimes built in their house so they could hide in it if anyone broke in.

Only, this safe room wasn't so safe.

Fin wondered if the irony of what he had done was lost on Pete.

As they approached, they saw light spilling out the open door. From inside they heard a grunt of pain, and he tried to run forward, only to be yanked back by Tom, who frowned at him.

Glaring back, he allowed the FBI agent to go first.

"Pete."

The man looked up at them. He was on the floor, struggling to drag himself to his feet, using an examination table for support.

Chloe was on the table.

Her skin was paper pale, and pain was written all over her face.

They were too late.

Pete Larkin had already hurt her.

She turned toward them and relief washed over her.

"Put your hands on your head, Mr. Larkin," Tom ordered.

The man ignored them and continued his struggle to stand but seemed to be having trouble controlling one of his legs, which kept giving out. Something had clearly happened to his leg, but Fin had no idea what. He did know that whatever it was, it had Chloe's name written all over it.

His girl would never go down without a fight.

"I'm not done," Pete Larkin muttered.

"Yes, you are," Tom said firmly. "Put your hands on your head."

It didn't look like Pete intended to go down without a fight.

Fin wanted to go running to Chloe. He might have if Tom wasn't blocking the doorway, preventing him from getting past.

He could feel her pain as though it were his own. She was struggling to remain conscious, and it was killing him that he didn't know how badly she was hurt—that he couldn't fix it.

He was a doctor; fixing people was what he did.

But he hadn't been able to fix his son, and now he couldn't fix Chloe.

"You're not walking out of this room except in handcuffs, Mr. Larkin. You are going to prison. You may as well just give yourself up now. Don't make it worse."

Pete stared at them.

It looked like he was contemplating doing as Tom had ordered him.

It wasn't like he had a lot of choices.

There was no way he was getting out of this.

Just when it looked like Pete was going to play things smart and surrender, he picked up a hammer that was lying on the floor beside him and threw it at Tom.

Tom fired a single shot.

Pete dropped.

Fin shoved past Tom and ran to Chloe.

Her eyes were closed, her color bad, sweat dotting her forehead. "Chloe?" He brushed the back of his hand across her cheek.

"Fin?" Her eyes opened slowly, then fell closed, before opening again even slower than the first time.

"I'm right here," he promised. He leaned over and kissed her forehead, then pressed his fingertips to her wrist to take her pulse. It was weak and erratic. Just as Savannah's had been when he'd treated her on the floor of Taylor's parents' house. And just like Savannah, it looked like Chloe had a broken bone. Her arm was swollen, red and already bruising. Pete had hit her with the hammer, breaking her humerus.

Tom appeared beside them and began to untie the straps that bound Chloe to the table. "Avery and Taylor are okay."

"Fin?" Taylor called out.

He knew that she wanted him, but right now Chloe was his only concern. "Chlo? Are you hurt anywhere other than your arm?"

"No," came the soft reply; pain laced her voice, and all he wanted to do was pick her up and hold her and make everything better.

"Are you sure?" She looked like she was going into shock so she could have other injuries she wasn't aware of.

She gave him a small smile that eased some of his worries. "I'm sure, Fin."

"You scared me to death. When I found you unconscious at Taylor's parents' house, my heart stopped. Then when I woke up and you were gone …" He trailed off. He couldn't even verbalize those feelings without them coming flooding back.

"I'm okay. I promise." She reached for him with her good hand and found his, interlacing their fingers.

Tears filled his eyes.

He had almost lost her.

Now he had her back, but he wanted all of her back.

He wanted her to be his again.

He wanted to be hers again.

"I need to splint your arm," he told her. Before he could get overwhelmed, he needed to do something that didn't require him to think. For the next few minutes, he was able to hold it together. He managed to tune out Chloe's pitiful whimpers as he put the splint on.

When he was done, he just stared at her.

There was so much he wanted to say.

So much he wanted to tell her.

But right now, there was only one thing that seemed too important to wait.

Although he knew he shouldn't move her, he gathered her into his arms and held her as tightly as he dared.

"I'm so sorry. For everything. I love you, Chloe."

She nestled her head against his neck and wrapped her good arm around his shoulders. "I love you, too, Fin."

The tears he'd been holding back earlier began to flow.

* * * *

6:13 P.M.

She was definitely ready to go home.

A couple of hours in the hospital and she was already going stir crazy.

Chloe was feeling much better. She had been poked and prodded and x-rayed and examined. Her broken arm didn't need surgery. It would heal on its own, but she was going to be wearing a sling for a good few weeks to keep her arm immobilized while the bone healed. She'd been given painkillers, and now the pain in her arm was nothing more than a dull, distant nuisance.

One of the first things she'd asked upon being rescued was about Savannah. Thankfully, her friend was alive, but it sounded like she had a long road of recovery ahead of her. And there was a possibility that she might never walk again. Chloe was devastated for Savannah, who had already been through so much. Still, at least she was alive, and there was hope.

Now she was sitting here, perched on the edge of her hospital bed, waiting for Fin.

Finally, they were in a place where they could work things out. They were on the same page. They loved each other, they were both sorry for the mistakes they had made, and they were ready to fix things between them.

So, where was he?

He'd held her in his arms back at Pete Larkin's house until the paramedics had arrived. Even then, he had only reluctantly handed her over to them. He'd held her good hand in the ambulance and stayed by her side in the ER. He had still been sitting in a chair beside her bed when her exhausted body had given out, and she had finally drifted off to sleep.

But when she'd woken up, he'd been gone.

That was over an hour ago, and he still hadn't come back.

A tiny flicker of doubt crept in.

Had he changed his mind?

She didn't doubt that he loved her, he had come looking for her, he'd been terrified for her.

That was the problem.

Had he only apologized to her because he'd been afraid of losing her?

Maybe he didn't really want to get back together.

The door to her room whooshed open, and she was almost afraid to look up and see who was there in case it wasn't Fin.

Or in case it was.

Fiddling with the hem of her sling, Chloe chanced a look up. It was Fin. He was standing in the doorway looking awkward.

"You can come in," she said, suddenly nervous.

"I just wanted to say goodbye." He took one uncertain step into the room.

Her stomach dropped. "Goodbye?"

"Not forever," he quickly clarified. "I just thought it might be better if your parents come and pick you up. I thought we should take some time. Maybe talk sometime in the new year. Once all of this …" He waved his hands in the air, and she assumed he meant everything that'd happened the last few days, "Has died down."

She knew what he was doing.

He was running away.

Again.

There was a time when she would have let him. She would have thought that she deserved everything he threw at her.

But those days were over.

"If you walk out that door, then it is definitely over between us, Fin," Chloe warned. And she meant it. She wasn't going to do this back and forth dance indefinitely. "So, you think carefully before you leave. I can't keep doing this. I can't take you blaming me and punishing me any longer."

Fin froze and looked at her, clearly confused. "Blaming you for what? Punishing you because you left me? I'm sorry about that, Chloe. I shouldn't have. I know you walked away because you were grieving."

"Blaming me for our son's death," she said quietly, dropping her gaze to the floor.

He said nothing.

Which hurt more than him admitting it out loud.

He didn't want to blame her because he still loved her, but he felt how he felt—there was nothing he could do about it. He was still too angry with her. Like he'd told her before; he still loved her, but they just couldn't be together.

"It's okay, Fin. I blame myself, too. I was his mother. It was my job to protect him, to keep him safe, but I didn't. I put him in danger with my job. I didn't want to give it up because I was pregnant. I even wished that I wasn't. And then I got my wish. He died. I don't deserve to be a mother. I'm sorry that I took your son from you. If I could take it back, I—"

"Stop!" Fin yelled.

Startled, her lips snapped closed, and she shrank away from him. He was angrier than she'd thought. Now that she was safe and he didn't have to worry about her, he couldn't hide it.

"Why are you saying such ridiculous things?" He stalked over to her and grabbed her shoulders, shaking her roughly and causing pain to shoot through her injured arm.

"I'm sorry," she said helplessly, unsure what else to say.

"Stop saying that. Stop apologizing to me. It's my fault." He released her and strode to the window, staring out it. "It's *my* fault," he said again, quieter this time.

Chloe didn't know what he was talking about. How could their baby's death have been his fault? He wasn't even in the car when she had the accident.

"I should have driven you to work that day," Fin continued. "You didn't like to drive in the rain. Maybe if I'd been driving, there wouldn't have been an accident. But even if there was, I should have saved him. I'm a doctor. It's my job to save people. But I failed him, and I failed you. I failed the two people I love the most."

"No," she said firmly. She went to him and wrapped her good arm around his waist, pressing herself against his stiff back. "It wasn't your fault, Fin. It wasn't."

He turned around and gave her a sad smile. "It wasn't yours, either."

"My head knows that's true, but my heart still blames myself."

His blue eyes crinkled in puzzlement. "Why would you blame yourself?"

"Are you really that stupid? Sorry, I don't mean stupid, but are you?"

"I really don't know why you would blame yourself. I was angry with you for leaving, but I never once blamed you for our son's death."

She wanted to believe that.

She really did.

"I thought you did."

Fin wrapped his arms around her and drew her close against his chest, being careful to not put pressure on her broken arm. His arms around her were strong and secure, making her feel safe and protected and loved. "Because I treated you so badly. I'm so sorry, Chloe. I don't deserve your forgiveness, but I'm asking for it."

"I forgive you," she said immediately. It was an easy forgiveness to give. The anger he had directed at her—for whatever reasons—still hurt, but you forgave the people you loved. "I'm sorry, too. For walking away instead of giving us the opportunity to grieve and heal together."

He looked at her with an inscrutable expression for so long that she started to squirm. Then he stooped and pressed a tender kiss to her forehead, then his lips hovered above hers, but he didn't kiss her. Instead, he said, "I forgive you."

Now, he kissed her.

Long and deep and passionately, stealing her breath as it went on and on.

So much emotion passed between them. Love, forgiveness, understanding. They had shared the greatest loss a couple could and finally it had brought them back together.

Tears filled her eyes, and when Fin finally broke the kiss, she rested her head against his chest. "It was just an accident. We both need to accept it. If we keep feeling guilty, it's going to tear us apart. We have to let go of the guilt. I just don't know how."

"We'll help each other," Fin promised.

"Okay." It was like a weight lifted off her shoulders. It was a relief to admit everything that she had been thinking and feeling since their son died. It was a relief to have someone to help her bear the pain.

They were together now.

Forever?

She had to know.

She had to be sure that Fin wouldn't change his mind again.

"You're not going to shut me out again, are you?" Chloe could hear the vulnerability in her voice, but she didn't try to hide it. She needed Fin to know that she couldn't take him shutting down again.

Fin leaned back, lifting one hand to tuck her hair behind her ear, then his hand lingered on her cheek. "I can't promise you I won't lose my temper or get angry about something. But I promise you that whatever life throws at us, we are in it together." It was his turn to radiate vulnerability. "You're not going to walk away again, are you? The next time something goes wrong, you're not going to up and leave?"

Giving him the same honesty he had given her, she said, "I can't promise you that sometimes I won't need space or some time on my own. But I promise that I won't ever walk away again. Next time, we deal with things together."

His body relaxed at her promise, just as hers had relaxed at his.

It seemed like Charlie was right, after all. Sometimes things weren't as they seemed. She'd thought that Fin blamed her for the baby's death, but he hadn't—he had blamed himself, just as she had blamed herself.

But blame and guilt only brought them unhappiness.

Maybe forgiveness and acceptance would bring them happiness.

"Can I take you home?" Fin asked.

"I'd love that."

* * * * *

8:24 P.M.

Fin put his arms around Chloe's shoulders as they walked from the car parked in the driveway to the front door. She leaned into him easily, like seven months of anger and hostility and guilt had never happened.

Could things really be this easy?

Could they both let go of their guilt and make things work?

He wanted to believe that they could, but it was hard to believe that they could just slip back into the relationship they'd had before.

He wanted it to work, more than he had ever wanted anything else in his life. He had just been afraid that Chloe might think differently once things had calmed down. So, although he had stayed by her side while she'd been treated, he hadn't wanted her to feel like she *had* to take him back.

Fin knew that after the way he'd treated her the last few days, he didn't deserve her forgiveness. And he'd been worried that once things settled down and she was safe and no longer fighting for her life, that she would realize that and rethink wanting to get back together.

What he hadn't been prepared for was her confession that she blamed herself for their baby's death.

She had misinterpreted his shock for anger and babbled apologies at him.

He didn't want her apologies.

He had wanted to rip her pain right out of her body and make it his own.

His anger had probably helped to fuel her guilt, despite the fact the anger had nothing to do with blame over the baby's death.

But that was behind them now.

Now they were on the same page.

He had the woman he loved back. It felt surreal. Emotions clogged up inside him. He still hadn't gotten over the fear of not knowing where Chloe was and what was happening to her.

Fin wasn't sure he ever would.

Every time he let his mind wander, it went back to that safe room in Pete Larkin's house. He kept picturing Chloe tied to that table, just as they'd found her, with Pete slamming his hammer into her body over and over again until every single bone was broken.

"I'm okay, Fin," Chloe said, wrapping her good arm around his waist.

"Your humerus is fractured," he corrected.

"It'll heal, and that's all he did to me. Nothing else. I'm fine."

She said the words, but he heard the slight tremble in her voice. She was shaken. Which was normal, but Chloe saw it as a weakness. "It's okay to be afraid, Chlo."

"I was afraid I'd never see you again." Her voice wobbled, and she turned into him, pressing her face against his chest. "I was so angry at you for the way you treated me the last few days, but I love you, Fin. I *always* loved you. I hate that I hurt you. I wish I could take it back."

Mindful of her broken arm, he held her as tightly as he dared. "At the hospital when I said goodbye, I didn't mean forever. I just thought you might want some time to process everything. I knew I'd hurt you with the way I'd treated you recently. It's just that it was so much easier to be angry with you than it was to face the pain of losing him. I was selfish, but I won't ever do that again. From now on, you are my number one priority. Always."

Chloe snuggled closer, her hair tickling his nose. This, he could get used to pretty quickly. How had he ever lived without her? Why had he let so much time go without doing whatever it took to get Chloe back?

Fin picked her up and carefully balanced her as he unlocked the door and carried her down into the family room, setting her on the couch. "Do you want something to eat?"

She grabbed his hands as he released her and tangled their fingers together. "I'm not hungry. I had a sandwich at the hospital, and the drugs they gave me are doing a great job at masking the pain, but they've kind of taken my appetite along with them."

"Something to drink, then? Hot chocolate? Coffee? Water?" Fin wanted to fuss like a mother hen and take care of her.

"Hot chocolate, maybe," she replied, a small amused smile on her face as he reached behind her to fluff up some pillows and prop them up behind her, then settling her against them. "You're cute when you fuss like this."

He made a face, no twenty-eight-year-old guy wanted to be called cute for any reason. "I'll go make the drinks. Are you cold? Do you want me to grab …?" Fin was standing up, preparing to go to the kitchen, when his eyes fell on the stocking hanging on the mantle.

It was the one they had bought for their son last Christmas.

He remembered the day they'd bought it. Chloe had gone on a huge shopping spree, buying a dozen baby's first Christmas decorations, little Christmas onesies, and this stocking.

"You put it out," he said as he picked it up, his fingers tracing over the merry Christmas scene.

"I don't want to forget him." Chloe came to stand beside him, leaning her head against his shoulder.

"Never," he said firmly. "We will *never* forget him. He will always be a part of us. Even if we have half a dozen other kids, we won't forget about him; he'll always be our firstborn."

"Christopher," Chloe murmured.

"What?"

She tilted her head up to look at him. "That's what I wanted to name him. We hadn't decided on a name, and then after he was gone, it was too painful to talk about, but I wanted to name him Christopher."

Christopher.

It was perfect.

He had never had a specific name in mind for his son, and maybe this was why. Chloe had already chosen the right name.

"I love it, Chlo. It's a beautiful name." He leaned down and touched his lips to hers. "You should be resting. Come and sit back down and I'll make the hot chocolate. Maybe we can watch a Christmas movie, then go to bed. I'm staying here tonight, right?"

"Oh, yeah." A playful smile lit her face, and she wrapped her good arm around his neck and tugged him down, trailing a line of light kisses along his jaw, before nipping at his bottom lip. "Instead of hot chocolate and a movie, you want to go upstairs?"

Fin chuckled and tucked her hair behind her ear. "For sex? Chloe, we can't. You have a broken arm."

She pouted, looking ridiculously adorably sexy. "I'm hopped up on pain pills; I feel fine. Please, Fin."

The begging did it.

Just as she had known it would.

"I guess we can do other stuff, but no sex," he said firmly.

"Okay," Chloe readily agreed with a self-satisfied smirk. She knew she was going to get her way.

"You know you're going to be sore tomorrow," he said as he lifted her up.

She wrapped her legs around his waist and kissed him. "I don't care. It'll be worth every ache. I've missed you too much. I don't want to wait another minute."

He knew where her bedroom was from the other night and headed straight to it, laying her down on the bed. Fin was just as eager to do this as Chloe was. Seven months was a *long* time to be away from the person you loved.

Her hand was pulling needily at his shoulder, urging him down so she could kiss him. Fin trapped her hand against his chest. "Slow down." He grinned, teasing her with an impossibly light kiss.

"I can't." She squirmed restlessly beneath him. "I need you."

"And you'll have me." He touched his lips to the sensitive spot on her neck and teased it with his tongue.

Tantalizingly slowly, he kissed his way down her neck, then bypassed her chest. With her broken arm, getting the sweater off was going to be a slow and painful process, one that was going to pull both of them out of the moment and throw him back into protection mode.

Instead, his hands went to her hips, and he eased her pants down and tossed them on the floor. Then Fin couldn't help but laugh. His silly girl was wearing a pair of snowman panties. They had a huge snowman face right in the center, complete with big, round black eyes, a goofy smile, and a carrot nose.

Chloe saw him looking at the panties and grinned. "You like them?"

"Love them. But not more than I love you," he said as he slid the panties down her legs and tossed them to join her pants on the floor. Then he settled himself between her legs, intending to make up for lost time tonight and devour every last inch of his gorgeous woman.

Christmas Day might be tomorrow, but he was getting his Christmas gift a little bit early this year.

DECEMBER 25TH

10:27 A.M.

"Morning, sleepyhead."

"Morning," Chloe mumbled as she blinked open sleepy eyes.

"Merry Christmas." Fin leaned over and kissed her.

That woke her up. "It's Christmas." She beamed. She had been dreading the holidays for weeks, scared to face it and all the memories of magical Christmases past, and the loss of the dreams she'd had of her first Christmas with her son. But now that it was here, things were pretty close to perfect. She still wished that Christopher was here and that they were celebrating his first holiday season as a family, but at least she and Fin were on the road to working things out.

"It is." Fin smiled back at her. It was nice to see him smile again. Before last night, she hadn't seen him smile since the day before the accident. She was so glad the battering they had taken, both individually and as a couple, was easing up now.

And what better time to reconnect than Christmas.

"How's your arm feeling?"

The pain had crept back in during the night. Invading her nightmares. Fin had woken her around midnight because she'd been crying in her sleep. He'd given her some more painkillers and gone through the whole doctor examination routine. She'd let him because she knew he needed to do it. He needed to take care of her right now; it was his way of showing her he cared.

The drugs must still be in her system and working their magic because she felt fine. Better than fine. She felt great.

"We should get up, get ready for church," she said, stretching, and snuggling up against Fin's warm body.

"We missed church," Fin told her, wrapping an arm around her and dragging her closer until she was half draped across his chest.

"We missed church?" She loved the Christmas service at the church she had attended since she was a baby. "What time is it?" She tried to look over Fin's shoulder to the clock on the nightstand.

"Ten-thirty."

"Why didn't you wake me?"

"Because you needed the rest," he reminded her. "Despite the fact you think you're doing fine, you know what happened has taken a toll on your mind and your body. You need rest."

Chloe knew he was right. Relaxing back against Fin, she absently trailed her fingers up and down his bare chest. "What are we doing today?"

Sure, she and Fin were back together, but were they telling people?

Were they waiting until they'd settled back into their relationship?

Whose family were they going to spend Christmas with?

Or were they going to spend the day just the two of them?

"Lunch with your parents and dinner with my sister." Fin answered like there was no other option.

"Same as last year." Things had slipped so easily back into the same routine they'd had before.

Suddenly, a strong hand snapped around hers. "You go any lower, and I'm not going to be able to give you your gift."

She looked down at her hand and saw that it had subconsciously been dipping lower and lower. She laughed and propped her chin on his chest. "Maybe you can just give me a different gift."

He lifted her hand and kissed her palm and then the inside of her wrist, making her shiver. "We can do more of that after. But I have something I really want to give you."

How did he have a gift for her? They had gotten back together only a little over ten hours ago—certainly not enough time for him to have gone shopping and bought her a present. "You really have something for me?"

"Just a little something I'd bought before we broke up. And even when things ended—I don't know, I just couldn't get rid of it."

He was looking at her so tenderly that her eyes couldn't help but mist over. The drugs sure were making her emotional. That or she was just deliriously happy to be alive and back with the man she loved.

"Wait right here." He gave her a quick kiss then gently eased her off his chest, carefully helping her sit and propping pillows up against the headboard for her to rest against.

While she waited for Fin to come back with his gift, she reached over to get the sling from the nightstand. She hated wearing it, but it did seem to help keep her arm in a comfortable position. And she thought that once it started to feel better, she was going to be tempted to start using it too soon. The sling should help with that too.

"Don't bother with that," Fin told her as he came back into the bedroom.

"With the sling? I thought I was supposed to wear it." Chloe had thought that Fin would be the main advocate of her following to the letter all the medical instructions she'd been given.

Fin shot her a mischievous grin. "You are, but I know how you love your goofy Christmas clothes, so I thought this one might be more fun for you to wear." He held out a brightly colored piece of material. It was covered in Christmas characters. Santa and Mrs. Claus, reindeer and snowmen, elves and presents, and little Christmas trees.

Chloe laughed. This was the weirdest, funniest, sweetest, most thoughtful gift she had ever gotten. It made her love Fin so much more. She knew he got embarrassed by her crazy Christmas outfits, but he never complained and was always buying her new things to add to her collection.

"Here, I'll help you put it on."

As Fin slid the material under her elbow and tied it around her neck, she waited eagerly to see what the gift was that he had for her. She had only broken her arm yesterday, so the sling wasn't the gift he had been talking about.

"You ready?" he asked as he leaned back against his heels on the bed.

She rolled her eyes at him. "You know I am." Fin knew darn well that she was notoriously bad at waiting to open gifts.

"I hope you like it." There was a hint of doubt in his blue eyes as he handed her a black velvet box.

It was a jewelry box.

But too big to be an engagement ring, so she knew he wasn't proposing.

Chloe opened the box and gasped.

"Oh, Fin. It's gorgeous," she gushed.

Inside the velvet box, nestled against a white piece of satin, was the most gorgeous gold locket she had ever seen. It was engraved with her name and Fin's, inside a heart, with a delicate garland of flowers circled around it.

It was beautiful.

It was perfect.

"Open it up."

At Fin's instruction, she picked the locket up and snapped it open. Then she gasped again.

Inside was a picture of Christopher.

They didn't have many. Just the sonogram ones from before he was born, and a couple they'd taken at the hospital in the few minutes he had lived.

Fin had chosen one of them and put it inside.

"Do you like it? I wasn't sure if you'd want a picture of

Christopher in there. I mean, that's what I originally intended. But then he died. When I decided last night to give it to you, I was going to leave it empty. But since you put up his stocking and the baby's first Christmas decorations on the tree, I thought maybe you'd like it. So, I asked Samara to bring a picture when she brought the locket and the sling. If you want, you can take—"

She scrambled awkwardly onto her knees and broke off his nervous rambling by crushing her mouth against his. When her lungs started screaming for air, Chloe ended the kiss and rested her forehead against his. "I love it. It's perfect."

"Just like you." His hands cupped her face, his thumbs brushing across her cheekbones.

"I'm not perfect," she reminded him. They had both made mistakes, and if they were going to learn from them and not repeat them, then they had to accept them.

"Okay." He smiled. "You're not perfect, and neither am I. But we're human, and we love each other, and that's pretty perfect."

Chloe couldn't agree more.

Life may not be perfect, but it was pretty close.

Jane has loved reading and writing since she can remember. She writes dark and disturbing crime/mystery/suspense with some romance thrown in because, well, who doesn't love romance?! She has several series including the complete Detective Parker Bell series, the Count to Ten series, the Christmas Romantic Suspense series, and the Flashes of Fate series of novelettes.

When she's not writing Jane loves to read, bake, go to the beach, ski, horse ride, and watch Disney movies. She has a black belt in Taekwondo, a 200+ collection of teddy bears, and her favorite color is pink. She has the world's two most sweet and pretty Dalmatians, Ivory and Pearl. Oh, and she also enjoys spending time with family and friends!

To connect and keep up to date please visit any of the following

Amazon – http://www.amazon.com/author/janeblythe
BookBub – https://www.bookbub.com/authors/jane-blythe
Email – mailto:janeblytheauthor@gmail.com
Facebook – http://www.facebook.com/janeblytheauthor
Goodreads – http://www.goodreads.com/author/show/6574160.Jane_Blythe
Instagram – http://www.instagram.com/jane_blythe_author
Reader Group – http://www.facebook.com/groups/janeskillersweethearts
Twitter – http://www.twitter.com/jblytheauthor
Website – http://www.janeblythe.com.au

sic enim dilexit Deus mundum ut Filium suum unigenitum daret ut omnis qui credit in eum habeat vitam aeternam

Made in the USA
Monee, IL
22 November 2021